They say there's a library at the end of the world.

After the final war comes the Cold. Humanity struggles to survive in the frozen wasteland they've made of the world, squabbling for resources and jumping at shadows. So much has been lost – it's only a matter of time before we lose the rest.

But there's a fragment of civilization left. Urban legends about The Collection, a sanctuary of knowledge which appears where it's most needed. And the stories about those who guard it are even stranger...

Dearest Maria,
Thanks you for the
support!

Read This
First

love [signature]

Edited by AC Macklin

Illustrated by Andrea Cradduck

CONTENTS

FOREWORD

by Andrew Knighton

Andrew Knighton is a freelance writer who gets to craft other people's stories for a living. He also writes his own stories, many of which can be found at andrewknighton.com. His collection is far less impressive than The Collection, far more focused on historical oddities and comics.

The best sources of inspiration are like barbed wire. They provide a boundary, a constraint to work within, something that focuses us on making the most of what we've got. And they provide barbs - those jagged, unexpected points that snag at our imaginations and tug threads loose for us to follow.

In that way – and that way only – AC Macklin is like barbed wire. Or maybe more like the rancher spooling out barbed wire around the field, fencing off a creative space for others to work within. She's the perfect collaborator, someone who gets you fired up then leaves you to run free with your dreams. Whether she's running a game or writing a story or arranging a trip to go ride the rollercoasters, she brims over with glee as she drags you into her tangle of barbed wire and shows you what an exciting place it can be.

Just look at *Read This First*, the story that starts this collection. It's full of barbs to hook the imagination on, from people to places to a tiger who might – just might – be your friend. Many of these barbs are provided in passing. All have blanks to be filled. They are the starting points for spectacular stories.

But there's a constraint too. The glorious constraint of writing about a library in a world that's fallen to pieces. The theme of imagination and inspiration and how vital that is to survival. The challenge of working to fill a world that others are writing in.

And what a world they've created! There are stowaways and strangers, dreams of dancers and the mysteries of monsters, all brought together by Andrea Cradduck's beautiful illustrations. These are stories of hope amid the darkness. But the stories and the pictures themselves hold out hope amid our darkness, reminding us that, however harsh the world seems, there is still beauty.

"Dreams let us imagine something better", AC Macklin says in *Read This First*. In that sense, she has shown that she is a dream.

A dream of barbed wire.

READ THIS FIRST

by AC Macklin

AC Macklin writes fantasy novels and short stories. She lives and works in London, whilst studying for an M.A in Creative Writing at Middlesex University. She has several short stories published in various anthologies. Her weekly blog on fiction writing can be found at www.everwalker.wordpress.com.

Day 1

Okay, first off, welcome to The Collection. Yes, it's not just a myth. But then, if you shlepped all the way out here (coz I'm leaving it in as remote a place as I can find to limit any potential fallout damage), you must've been pretty confident about that.

There's a little bit of a cubby area just to the right of the entrance. I'll put water and some protein bars there. You're probably in need of them. Keep this book with you. It's the only form of handover you're going to get. Sorry about that. I would've loved to stick around and meet you but, well, I'm not going to make it.

Right, introductions. My name's Tia and my family looked after The Collection for a while. It isn't quite like the legends say. It doesn't have every book ever written, for a start, and the layout stays the same. It's just the front door that moves, but only on the outside. Once you're in there's a map on the wall by the coat-rack.

It does have a lot of books, and also tons of music and art from before the Cold. When the war was gearing up a bunch of people spent time and money on how to send the rich into the relative safety of space. Others prepared for surviving the nuclear winter. And a couple of crazies focused on saving as much art as they could. I don't know why, you'd think there were bigger problems to worry about, but here we are. The world's last library.

Oh, and there's a vegetable garden in the basement. You'll need to look after that.

See, here's the deal. You guard The Collection, stop folks stealing from it, share the knowledge where it's needed, add to it as and when you can. In return, it'll give you someplace warm and dry and safe to live, with clean water and actual food grown in non-toxic soil. Pretty sweet, huh? Aren't you glad you hauled ass all the way out here?

But you have to do the job. It's important. We lost so much in the Cold and this place can help restore some of it. Help people survive. That's power, and plenty of bosses would love to get their hands on it. Control it, ration it, whatever. The Collection doesn't allow that. It's why the door keeps moving. It's not up to you, either. You help whoever needs it, no matter what. We're too good at forgetting we're all in this mess together.

My dad made that mistake.

You're probably tired. If you head straight on, past the Agriculture section, there's a staircase up to the observatory. There's a bed there. It was mine but you can have it. I liked watching the colours of sunset in the ash. Rohini usually sleeps there too. Please look after him. I think he's going to miss me.

That's my deal. I wrote this to help you, but you have to look after my cat. Please.

Day 2

I hope you had a good sleep. The bathroom's in the basement. You'll need to take the lift, which is just behind the armillary sphere. The water's always warm - it uses hot springs or fault lines or something. I left you a towel down there.

I can still remember my first shower here, back when Dad brought us in. I hadn't realised it was possible to feel so clean. There wasn't any soap then, of course, but Mum found a recipe in one of the herbalist books in Section 615.3. There's a couple of bars left of the last batch. Sorry about the smell - I burned the mint. But hey, soap!

There should be enough non-perishable food in the kitchen for a couple of weeks, until you've found your feet. That's just off the bathroom. I think the designers figured they'd put all the potentially leaky stuff at the bottom, so if there was an accident with the pipes it wouldn't damage the Collection.

Oh, yeah, it's a minor point but I've always thought of it as the contents is the Collection and the structure itself is The Collection. Powerful enough that it deserves both capital letters, right? I don't know if you're the kind of person who cares about that sort of thing.

Anyway, breakfast. Rohini will have whatever you're having. If he hasn't made an appearance yet, just leave some out on the table. He'll find it. He's probably watching you from a distance, deciding whether you're safe. A lot of people aren't, but I guess you already know that. I found him in a shanty-town somewhere in Uttarakhand. They'd kept him in this tiny cage and shaved him over and over to use his fur for warm clothes. So you'll understand if he doesn't immediately make friends with new people. Dad wanted to call him Dewey but I thought that was too easy.

You won't know the Dewey Decimal System yet but it's pretty important. Every subject has a numerical code, and the books are all marked with the appropriate one and filed together. Each class (each group of subjects which share the same first number, so everything religiony starts with a 2, for example) has it's own floor in The Collection. So there's ten floors of books (because 0 is a number) plus the DNA bank, the art gallery, the observatory, and the basement. Dad used to make my sister and me recite the classes every morning over breakfast. He said if we knew our way around Dewey we could never get lost. I guess he was wrong about that.

By the way, if you're wondering whether you're going to trip over my corpse at some point, don't worry. I know what's coming for me and I don't think they'll do things that way. I'd be lying if I said I wasn't scared, but I'm so tired of running. I've got time to finish the filing, write this up, maybe have a final bowl of blackberries if the harvest comes through before they get here.

I'm guessing you've never tasted blackberries. They're the best food ever. Tiny clouds of silky skin that bulge against your tongue before bursting into mild sweetness, or tart sweetness, and always so fresh you can practically taste the sky above the ash. I bought Rohini for a carton of blackberries.

The garden's on the basement level too. Don't ask how it grows down there, I don't know. There's a whole bunch of stuff I could never figure out the mechanics of. I guess it's part of the tech we lost the knowledge of, from before the Cold. I can't find it written up in the Collection. That always made me a bit nervous because, if it broke, I didn't know how to fix it. But it's never broken.

Anyway, go have a wander. I recommend taking a flask of water with you, and there's a ball of red string in the kitchen to keep you from getting lost. It's a big place and you don't know Dewey yet.

Day 3

It feels weird, not knowing your name or what you'll look like. I'm going to think of you as Theseus. Dewey 398.2. Go look it up.

The minotaur should be long gone, by the way. They won't stick around to get you too. But without anyone keeping an eye on the place there's other things that may have snuck in. Don't think The Collection will protect you from physical danger. It isn't sentient or anything wacky like that, it's just a building with some unique physics. I assume you've got your own weaponry, given you made it here, but there's stuff stashed around the place as well. A lot of it is in The Collection because it's art or historical artefacts, but it's art made out of sharp metal so that's kinda the point.

Sorry. Bad pun. Sanna, my little sister, used to roll her eyes so hard I thought she was going to strain something but she loved my jokes really. She even laughed a couple of times. She had this high giggle that made me think of tiny bells. The first time I heard it I thought she was ill. This isn't a world for laughter but The Collection helps kids be kids instead of miniature survivors. Not just kids, either.

That's what Class Eight is for. (We call the floors 'classes' - it cuts down on the confusion.) In a world this broken you might think there's not much point to fiction, but you're wrong. I've been places - desperate, starving, clinging-on-by-their-fingertips places - where the book about fairies did nearly as much good as the book about water filtration. It gives people a break, reminds them how to dream. Dreams let us imagine something better, and if we can't do that things will never improve. Mum used to say it was nonsense, a waste of time, but Dad understood.

I keep telling myself that. He was just trying to make things better. But you have to go about it the right way. Don't steal, Theseus. If there's something you need, or something The Collection is missing, you barter for it. Knowledge, food, a hot shower, there's plenty to barter with here. You don't have to steal. Especially not from beings that can track The Collection door.

See, the other thing about the books on Class Eight? Not all of them turned out to be fiction.

Day 4

It's probably time to explain the front door. Go up to the observatory. There's a big red curtain covering a section of wall next to the lift - pull it to one side. See all those brass dials and cogs? I have absolutely no idea how they work. Dad said the mechanism is called an antikythera. He got very excited when he first saw it. Apparently this is the only time anyone's got it to work, ever.

There's an oil-can tucked away in an alcove at the bottom. You'll need to drop a bit on each of the cogs whenever they start to squeak. Trust me, you don't want this thing breaking down. The Collection would get stuck and being static is a bad thing. All those bosses I said would love to get their hands on this much knowledge? Yeah, they'd find you inside of a month. The Collection might be a legend to most people but enough of them believe that there's plenty of informants out looking. Never stay anywhere longer than two weeks, is my advice.

I really hope you got here within a couple of weeks of me going, otherwise Rohini's going to make a horrible mess. Has he come out to say hello yet? He's surprisingly good at hiding, for something so big and orange. I think it's the stripes.

Anyway, the big winding handle on the side of the machine is how you move the door. You need to crank it all the way round at least once. I usually give it a couple of turns, just in case. There's another in a little cupboard by the front door, in case of emergencies, but it's better if you use the main one. The cogs seem to jam up after using the emergency handle.

That'll move the door, and if you can figure out how to control where it moves the door to then you're doing better than we ever managed. Sanna used to say it took us to wherever The Collection was needed the most, but that makes it sound like it's sentient. I promise you it isn't. Yellow Hat told Dad it isn't, and I believe it.

The door will end up anywhere there's an empty rectangular space for it. That isn't always convenient for you. We came out behind a waterfall once. This is where it gets properly weird, though. The Collection is attached to the door, and the door is attached to wherever its new frame is, but The Collection isn't attached to the frame. The door ended up on the side of a freight carriage recently but I'm very sure the entirety of The Collection wasn't sticking out the side of the train. That's where I saw Yellow Hat for the first time, that train. I'll tell you more about it tomorrow.

Come on, The Collection's been in one place too long already. Get your gear ready and turn the handle. And when you go out, remember where you left the door!

Day 5

How was your trip? I wonder where you ended up, and if you could understand the language. Ooh, I wonder if you can even read this? I never thought of that. I'll make copies in other languages if I have time.

Did you find people who needed help? I shouldn't think you had to look very far. Nearly everyone needs help these days. And once you start giving it, it becomes addictive. I tried to leave once. Snuck out whilst everyone was asleep and ran for hours, with Rohini trotting along next to me. This was somewhere in England, I don't remember exactly where. I found this row of tall brick houses with long thin gardens. All the houses were full, of course, but one of the gardens had space at the bottom for another person. I put a tarp over a piece of rope and called it home. Rohini wasn't impressed but he stuck around, which kept me from freezing. I lasted five whole days. Sanna thought it was the snow that made me come back, and Mum thought it was the people. (I got a bloody nose and a black eye, and it would've been a lot worse only they weren't expecting a tiger.) But it wasn't.

I hope you're a helper, Theseus. There aren't many with the means to do it, and it's so easy to be selfish in the Cold. Which is why it's important not to be.

I said I'd tell you about Yellow Hat. That's why I ran away. If I'd known more then, I wouldn't have bothered. Running just wears you down. It's alright, though. You're safe. This is about Dad's bloodline, not yours. That isn't the right name, by the way. More of a description. A tatty mustard-yellow hat with a huge brim, and a big dirty coat that Mum said is called camel-hair but isn't actually made out of camels. And white gloves. Who wears white gloves? They get dirty the moment you set foot outside. But Yellow Hat's gloves always looked clean.

Dad said his real name was Kaiwan, but to always call him 'sir'. Mum said things like him didn't have a real name, or a gender to go with it. I thought at the time she was being sharp because Dad was late for dinner again and she didn't like the place we were at. The front door came out in a little stone hut near the Dead Sea, built for shepherds, Dad said. Sanna and me thought it was great. We spent a whole afternoon splashing about trying to get under the surface of the water whilst Rohini rolled in the mud. Mum wasn't too happy about that either. I cleaned it all off but she still yelled at me. Looking back, I think she needed something safe to yell about.

Yellow Hat was a local boss. He'd got his territory pretty well set up. There was farming and clean water, the whole works. But Dad said there was something wrong with the settlement. Nobody would talk to him, or even look at him. He said it was like everyone had gone away inside their heads and were just doing things out of habit. Mum said people dealt with the Cold in their own way but he shook his head and said, not like this. Yellow Hat was the only person who talked. He figured out pretty quick that Dad was with The Collection, which panicked us all to start with, but apparently he was only interested in it in passing. He already knew everything useful in here, he told Dad, and a bunch of stuff that wasn't in here besides.

I heard Dad and Mum talking about it in the kitchen, when I came in from washing the mud off Rohini. He said he'd asked Yellow Hat to barter for this new knowledge but the boss would only pat his battered leather briefcase and say 'the souls of your family for everything I know'. Dad tried to pass it off as a joke but Mum went quiet for a bit. Then she used her this-is-my-final-word-there-will-be-no-argument voice and told Dad we were moving first thing the next day.

Dad went out again after supper. He was gone for hours, so long that we all went to bed without him. I don't know how much later I got woken up but it was still dark. Dad was standing in front of the antikythera with a battered leather briefcase in his hand. He was breathing fast, like he'd been running. I sat up as he wound the handle half a dozen times, getting more jerky and frantic with each turn. When he turned around and saw me watching I thought he was going to yell at me.

"That's Yellow Hat's briefcase," I said. I'd never seen it before but somehow I knew.

"Tia, what are you doing still awake?"

"Did you barter our souls away?"

He sat down on the bed next to me and shook his head. "No, baby. I would never. I'm just borrowing it so I can make copies. He'll get it back."

He was right about that, anyhow.

Look, Theseus, the point is that searching for new knowledge is a good thing. The Collection needs to be added to. Ask questions, barter for new stuff, that's part of the job. But you have to come by it honest.

Day 6

Okay, lending policy. I figure now you've been out and seen how much The Collection can help people, you'll have some questions about how this works. Pretty much all of the books here are irreplaceable. A lot of stuff went up in smoke when the Cold hit, and books burn easy. For all the people who'd want The Collection for its knowledge, there's just as many who want it for its fuel. So rule one is: don't let other people in. Rohini will help with that.

If you want to make an exception, you have to be absolutely completely sure they can be trusted. It's your life on the line, remember, not to mention all the thousands of people The Collection helps. There isn't some kind of vetting system, that's what human instinct is for.

Taking books outside, that's risky too. What if it gets lost, or stolen, or damaged by ash? They're fragile things, books. No, it's best to work out what knowledge the locals need, write some notes, and take those outside. You can always come back and look up more stuff.

Obviously that doesn't work for everything. Classes Seven and Eight need to be read by the person who needs them. So there's a lending policy. They have two weeks from when The Collection arrives to finish reading, and they have to leave something with you for surety. If they don't bring the book back, you go get it.

Mum was in charge of our late returns. When she was wielding a shotgun she could scare the crap out of me, and I was standing on the right side. It wasn't often we had that kind of trouble, though. The people who need books from Classes Seven and Eight tend not to be overly unscrupulous. The only time it got bad was on the freight train.

There was a whole community living there. Mostly doctors and mechanics and the like, with their families. They rode the tracks, bartering skills for food as they passed people. They were scraping by, doing okay. Doing better than many. They didn't need The Collection for agriculture, or building, or any of the normal stuff. They needed Class Eight for their kids. We stayed there the full two weeks.

The day everything was due back in, no one came knocking so we went to find out what the problem was. All the kids said this guy had taken their books off them. Tall, thin, cousin of one of the train drivers. He'd been ripping the pages out and bartering them individually as kindling, toilet paper, smokes, a fragment of story, whatever people would pay for. Of course the kids didn't rat to us - he was one of their own, even if he was a douchebag, and we were strangers. Anyway, Mum tracked him down and gave her you-owe-us-and-I've-come-to-collect speech which ought to have had him pissing himself with fear.

He laughed in her face. Said he'd heard of The Collection before and he knew we had something way more valuable than books. Something that didn't belong to us. He'd sent word to Yellow Hat the day we arrived. Which was deeply worrying, but we were on a different continent to the Dead Sea and travel isn't exactly easy anymore, not when you don't have an antikythera.

Then Dad freaked. He grabbed the guy by the throat and started shaking him, yelling in his face about betraying his own species, and what else did he know? Everyone around us got antsy at that stage. They weren't inclined to stand back and watch as this crazy stranger throttled their neighbour. Mum ended up firing into the roof so they'd stay back. Sanna and me grabbed Dad by the elbows and we hustled back to The Collection. Mum had the cupboard for the emergency handle open before I'd even closed the door.

The last thing I saw of that train was the freight carriage with everyone backing up around the sides. Yellow Hat was walking slowly towards us, like he had all the time in the world. I swear he was smiling.

Never did get those books back.

Day 7

Now that you've settled in a bit, you're probably wondering what the big flat screens in 770 are for. Dad said they were called 'computers', and they were how everything worked before the Cold. You can read all about them in 000, if you're interested. They were put into The Collection to play the music library, and something called films which were stories acted out and recorded. But the fuel they used stopped working when the Cold happened, so now they're basically useless. Mum called them 'museum pieces'.

I guess, if you're older than me, you already know some of this. Maybe you remember before the Cold. I was a baby when it happened, and Sanna wasn't quite born, so the world has always been this way to me but my parents used to reminisce about how things were. How everyone could be warm whenever they wanted, and food grew easy, and you didn't have to test for water acidity before you drank it. Mum said there was no ash in the air, then. Sometimes she sat on the end of my bed at night and stared out of the observatory dome. When I asked her why, she said she was remembering stars. She told me stories about animals that lived in the sky - a lion, and a giant crab, and a bear. They didn't fly, they were made of starlight. Did you ever see them, Theseus?

She stopped telling stories after Dad opened Yellow Hat's briefcase. A lot of things stopped then. Dad stopped sleeping. I don't mean insomnia, I mean at all. His skin went very pale and his eyes went very bloodshot. He couldn't stay still, always tapping his foot or drumming his fingers. He muttered constantly, until Mum screamed at him to shut up, just shut up. After that, he whispered. I think the whispering was worse. Like rustling pages, turning over too fast to make out the words. At least when he was talking I could hear what he said, even if it didn't make much sense.

He talked about the Cold, how it didn't come from the war. Or it did but the war wasn't really started by us. He said something from behind the stars made us turn the world into ash and ice. Kaiwan was just waiting for humans to die out, enjoyed watching it happen slowly. He told Mum the people in Yellow Hat's settlement were already dead but they weren't allowed to stop. That's when she screamed at him.

A few days later the front door opened onto the deck of a metal ship, tipped crazy by pack-ice. Dad walked out into the dark, barefoot, and didn't come back. Mum waited twenty-four hours. Then she turned the handle.

Day 8

Dad's boots are under the coat rack. You can have them, if you like. There's a good few years of wear left in them, if you repair the inner seam on the left one. You'll get good at repairing things here, if you aren't already. Like I said before, books are fragile things, especially when they're old. Spines crack, stitching comes loose, and no one else is going to fix it.

All the stuff is in the workshop on Class 0. First you'll need to remove the damaged cover with a sharp blade. Use the piece of straight wood to make sure all the pages are lined up together, if they're loose, then clamp them tight. You might need to sew some of them back together - there's a sewing kit in the box. Make the holes first with the punch pliers. Don't pull the thread too tight or you'll tear the pages when you try to open the book. Cut the new cover out of leather, using the old one to get the size right. Put glue up the spine, wrap it round the pages and clamp it all together for a day.

Sanna was really good at fixing books. She had clever fingers. That's what Dad used to say. "You've got clever fingers, baby," and she'd light up with pride. She was Dad's daughter - they had the same sensitivity, the same love of beauty and need for praise. Mum and me were the practical ones. Well, someone has to be. The Collection needs both kinds of people. Maybe that's why we were chosen in the first place.

The man who was here before us was one of the founders. He was very sick, or maybe he had been sick before the war, I'm not sure. He knew there weren't medicines any more to make it better, so he started searching for someone to take care of The Collection when he was gone. He looked for nearly a year before he found us. Mum and Dad were part of a group living in some caves in Greece. There wasn't enough food to go around - Dad was cutting his rations so Sanna and me could eat. She was barely walking then, but I could help carry water and watch the fires.

I don't remember the stranger arriving. First he wasn't next to my fire, and then he was. He had a nice smile so I wasn't afraid. He started talking to me, I don't remember what about, and Dad came running over to pull me away. The stranger held his hands wide, but he started coughing and folded in half. There was blood on his lips when he straightened up again. I remember that very clearly. It gleamed in the firelight.

He and Dad talked for a long time. Mum came back from fishing with Sanna and they all talked for even longer. Then Mum and Dad both cried a bit, and I helped Mum put everything we owned in a blanket. Dad was too weak to carry it, so Mum put it on her back and I took Sanna. We followed the stranger to the back of the cave, to a door I'd never seen there before. After that we were warm, and fed, and safe.

He died a few months later. We wrapped him in our old blanket and buried him on top of a mountain, like he wanted. Leibowitz, he was called. I don't have many memories of him, beyond a soft voice and a kind hand. We had to be careful when we touched him. His skin was so pale and thin, and bruised so easily. Towards the end he could hardly breathe for coughing. If he hadn't had The Collection, he would have died much earlier.

Sensitive people don't do well in the Cold.

Day 9

There's still places where the ground is sick from the war. If you stop at one of those, Rohini will snarl at the door before it's even opened. That's how you know about the sickness. There's a big yellow suit in a cupboard in the bathroom which lets you go out safely. It's worth it because there's usually something to save from those places. No one else scavenges there. Always make sure there's no holes in the suit before you go out, otherwise you'll get sick too. When you come back, shower in it really thoroughly, take it off and scrub it, and then shower again. There's a big safe on Class 0 to put scavenged things from those places - only open it when you're wearing the suit. They have to be kept locked up because they'll make you sick, but Mum said that after years and years the sickness will fade. The safe number is 29139.

The briefcase was in there for a time, after Dad opened it.

We went back. Not deliberately, it just happened that one turn of the handle took us to the shepherd's hut by the Dead Sea again. Mum said it was a sign. She told Sanna and me to stay inside, no matter what. She promised she'd be back in a couple of hours. Then she took the briefcase and left.

It got dark and she still hadn't come back. Sanna started to cry, saying she'd abandoned us, but I knew that wasn't true. She'd gone to barter because she loved us. We loved her, so we went after.

Yellow Hat's settlement was half an hour's walk, up a valley that must have had a river in it once. We came to fields first, full of crops that stood tall and weren't covered in snow. Shapes were moving through them, slow and silent. I put my hand over Sanna's mouth and we crouched at the edge, watching. It took me a long time to realise they were people. I opened my mouth to ask who farms at night, but then I remembered Dad saying they were dead, and I shut it again. We snuck around the edge and crept to where the buildings were. One of them - the biggest - had lamps still burning and the door open. The smell of hot food came from a window. It smelled just like Mum's Anything Curry. Sanna sniffed, then stood up and looked through the window. She gave a little cry and called out to Mum. I grabbed her by the wrist but there were already shadows moving towards the door.

Mum came out into the street. She looked at us and her face didn't change. I knew then what Dad had meant about the people here going away in their heads. Sanna tried to go to her, but I held her still. Then Yellow Hat appeared in the door. He was holding the briefcase in one hand and a steaming bowl of Anything Curry in the other. He smiled at Sanna and his teeth were too white.

I didn't let her stop running until we were back. I think she hated me for leaving Mum there. But there wasn't anything to bring home.

Day 10

In case you're wondering, there's no way to turn the lamps off. They're powered by thermal coils and my best guess is they tap into the same heat source as the hot water (wherever that is). It never bothered me - there's so much dark outside and it's not like they're especially bright - but Sanna used to bury her head right under the pillow to get to sleep.

They don't break often but very occasionally the metal wire will warp or snap. There's a coil in the workshop which should be enough for two lamps, but after that you'll need to barter for more. There's plenty of that kind of thing in the European settlements still. When you've got it, lift the lamp cover off - it comes easy, it's not secured to anything - and use the tiny screwdriver to release the old wire from the two clamps. Change it out for the new stuff, and replace the cover. Easy. The wire will heat up pretty quick though, so you can't ~~hang~~ mess around.

The left-hand lamp in the bathroom needs fixing. I couldn't. I'm sorry.

When you go into markets to barter, you need to not be too clean. It's an easy thing to forget. There's enough hot water for a shower every day, more than one if you want. But being clean's a sure way to mark you out as different. Privileged. At best, they'll make you pay way over the odds. At worst, they'll kill you. Being clean's reason enough in some places.

Also, don't go alone if you can help it. There's not many places are friendly to strangers. The last few times, when Sanna wouldn't leave The Collection, I went with Rohini. He doesn't like it, all the people and the noise, but he'll come if you take a treat with you. Rabbit's a favourite, and not too rare.

Sanna said she saw Yellow Hat at the market. It's why she wouldn't go out. Every market, anywhere we went, she said she saw him. Just out of the corner of her eye, or disappearing round a corner. I never caught a glimpse but she swore he was always watching. I didn't push, figured it was just a reaction to Mum going and she'd get over it eventually. But it got worse. After a couple of months she started seeing him inside The Collection. I knew that wasn't true - Rohini would have growled - but she refused to leave the workshop, where her bed was. Is. Still is.

I came back from helping design a waste drainage system for a small settlement, and heard her screaming. I thought she'd had an accident, broken a bone or burned herself. Broken bones don't necessarily mean death in The Collection but shock can still kill you. I dropped everything and ran to the workshop. She was curled up on her bed, pushed right up into the corner, with both hands pulling at her hair. I shouted at her, slapped her cheek, wrapped myself around her - nothing worked. In the end I used some of the morphine from the medicine cupboard. It's valuable but I didn't know what else to do. Finally she went limp. I tucked her up and brought my own blankets to sleep on the floor next to her. I didn't want her waking up alone.

It took me ages to drift off, and I felt like I'd only been out for a few hours before Rohini woke me up by headbutting my stomach. Sanna's bed was empty. She didn't answer when I called. Rohini was whining by the door, shifting from foot to foot. I followed him to the lift and he took me down to the basement. When he stands on his back legs he's tall enough to punch the buttons with his nose.

She was in the bathroom. The noose had broken the lamp. The metal in it was as cold as her.

I couldn't bear to fix it. I'm sorry.

Sanna, I'm sorry.

Day 11

I've left the front door open so Rohini can get in and out. He hasn't had much chance to hunt recently, what with all the running, and feeding him from bartered stuff gets expensive. He's not too keen on rat, but horse or rabbit are good treats if you can get them. I think there's quite good hunting round here so hopefully he'll be fine until you come. The door opens into a cave, so the snow doesn't come in, and most other animals will back off when they smell Rohini.

I wonder if he'll be lonely without me. Maybe he's already lonely. Sometimes I hear him roaring outside, a way off. There's never an answer. Perhaps there's no other tigers left in the world. Lots of things died in the Cold. There's copies of them downstairs in the DNA bank, but what good is that? Even if the tech to bring them back still existed, and the fuel to make it work, the world is too broken for them to survive in. The war didn't just take lives. It took the way of life.

The Collection is a memorial for everything that died. Including us.

You'd think, after the war, people would try harder to get along. But everywhere I've been, there's little fights and big fights and murder for no reason than because someone's different. Like we're not all dying slow anyway. Like fighting will fix anything. The world's ash and ice, and we've learned nothing. Worse than nothing. It's too easy to forget, these days.

The Collection has a real physical place, by the way. It doesn't just live in a weird pocket dimension, like some of the books on Class 8 talk about. It's inside a mountain in the Himalayas. We built Leibowitz's cairn on top, near the observatory window. It seemed right to bury him next to the thing he made. I go and sit there sometimes. He deserves to be remembered for what he did, even if it's only by one person.

You'll have to go back occasionally to wipe the snow off the dome. If you pull the handle of the antikythera so it's pointing straight out from the wall, then turn so it's facing down and push it flat again, the door will go there. You know what it looks like from the outside. That's where you came in.

Day 12

Yellow Hat is here. I didn't hear him arrive but I just looked up and there he is, standing under the observatory dome. Smiling. He hasn't said anything, only nodded when I asked for enough time to write this page.

I didn't finish the filing. Sorry. And I didn't wash up the dishes this morning. There was more I wanted to tell you, about Sanna, and the place in Koh Phangan where they still have pineapples, and how the seed catalogue works, and what to do when Rohini has toothache.

I thought I was ready. I'm not ready at all. I'm scared. I love this place. I don't want to leave it. I don't want to leave Rohini. You have to look after them both, Theseus. Please. Please love them both for me.

I wish I could've met you.

tia

14

SYMPTOMS

by Eleanor Loughton

Eleanor is a Highland lass who fell in love with the fields, hedge rows and ancient trees of England. By trade she is a mechanical design engineer, but she is happiest when immersed in an imaginary world. Even in those creative places however she is inspired by logic. She loves to watch the layers unfurl, in their infinite fascinating ways, when you ask the question 'why?'.

I could see the symptoms on her a mile off. She'd have stuck out to me even if she hadn't been accompanied by the tiger. Some said I had an unhealthy obsession with the Sickness but, the way I saw it, at least I was focussing my energies on trying to solve something, trying to help. Seemed better than venting it in anger and violence and jealously guarding the few scraps we had left. Actually, that's not fair. There are lots of wonderful people who have remained so despite the Cold. Survival tends to bring out undesirable traits, as well as making the generous ones seem even more precious.

The first thing that caught my eye was how she moved. Jumpy, tense, paranoid. Any stranger has reason to be jumpy but there's a particular type of skittishness that stands out from the others if you've seen it enough. A slight wildness, like the things they are scared of can't be seen by the rest of us.

I started following her. I hadn't seen anyone with the Sickness here since the travellers moved on, and the last people infected... ended, one way or another. As I got closer I could see that greyish translucent tint to her skin. That's when I knew she was quite advanced. She must have been hardy to still be able to travel. Most people stop functioning pretty quickly. Apart from Mr Jones – he got too close. He went the other way. Like some of the travellers. And Jane.

I followed this one back to her door. I admit, I was a little hesitant to actually go in there. I didn't know what might have infected her. But I was loathe to pass up the chance to learn more about it, to work towards a cure. No one else seemed to be doing it and I needed something to focus on. I needed to believe there was hope. I thought I might just fade away if all I did was survive, morsel by morsel, scrap by scrap.

The door felt more substantial than it looked. It moved, heavy and deliberate, on smooth hinges, reminding me of the doors to the chambers at work, before the Cold. Nothing runs that smoothly now. It made me pause. Inside was strangely quiet, insulated from the rest of the world.

The tiger came around the corner at the end of the corridor and I froze, heart racing. He slowly padded up to me, sleek muscles flowing over powerful shoulder blades, but just sniffed at my hands before walking away. It felt like I was back in a world where fat pet cats curled up in front of the fire, and walked around the house as if they owned the place. Except this was a much bigger cat.

I stayed hidden from her as long as I could. Watching as she pottered around, and wrote in her book, and moved the big handle on the machine in the observatory. I slowly realised she didn't really see me. She was too far gone. I thought maybe she'd be going the other way, like Mr Jones, especially as she was still sleeping on and off. But in the end that wasn't the case.

By the time a day had passed Jane, still back at home, was tugging at my conscience. But logically I knew she wouldn't really be missing me. Better to stay and piece together a few more bits of the jigsaw, I told myself. Find clues to navigate the solution.

I had only been in there for a few days when it happened. The sick girl looked up. And this time she saw me.

I'd rehearsed in my head what I would say if I was discovered. Tried to get it short enough, and convincing enough, that it might buy me some time. People are protective of their safe places, their resources, and this girl had more than I had thought possible. She didn't seem like the violent type but you can never be sure.

In the end I didn't need my carefully rehearsed words.

"Hello, Yellow Hat."

I turned, and there she was, looking at me. I'd lost track of her, just for a moment.

"Don't worry," she said "I'll come quietly, when it's time." And she walked away.

I was on edge for days, thinking she might be lulling me into a false sense of security. But it soon became clear that she thought she knew who I was. Someone she called "Yellow Hat". My 'hat', if any, was only a piece of black fabric wrapped around my head for warmth, not even a hat really. She never challenged me, just continued madly scribbling in that book of hers. It wasn't until the day she left that I realised it was part of her Sickness, part of the way she and her family had succumbed.

I grew bold. She was hardly sleeping anymore. Wouldn't do anything other than stare into space over her book, occasionally coming to life and writing a passage before returning to her vacant reverie. My curiosity got the better of me, and I dared stand where I could read over her shoulder. She looked up at me for a moment. My breath caught, but I chanced my luck and smiled. She went back to writing.

Yellow Hat is here. I didn't hear him arrive but I just looked up and there he is,

18

standing under the observatory dome. Smiling. He hasn't said anything, only nodded when I asked for enough time to write this page.

I didn't finish the filing. Sorry. And I didn't wash up the dishes this morning. There was more I wanted to tell you, about Sanna, and the place in Koh Phangan where they still have pineapples, and how the seed catalogue works, and what to do when Rohini has toothache.

I thought I was ready. I'm not ready at all. I'm scared. I love this place. I don't want to leave it. I don't want to leave Rohini. You have to look after them both, Theseus. Please. Please love them both for me.

I wish I could have met you.

Tia

She calmly put down her pencil. "Let's go, Yellow Hat."

Rising, she walked to the front door. It swung open, heavy on its hinges, and I gasped in a blast of snow-flecked wind. I couldn't quite fathom what had happened. Where was the grimy backstreet I had followed her down? Where was the town? For a moment fear washed over me. Had I succumbed to the Sickness? Before I could process what was happening she walked out of the door. Spurred into action I grabbed a coat from the rack and followed.

The cold took my breath away. The world seemed to contract around me as I squinted against the freezing flakes. Everything was white and grey and black. It was a mountainside. The occasional rock face loomed as a dark shape in the whirling white of the storm. Tia was fast disappearing into the blizzard so, in my confusion, I hunched my coat around me and followed.

I tried to shout after her but I don't know whether she heard me above the wind. We pressed on for long minutes. Suddenly she turned to look at me... and disappeared. I stumbled quickly forward.

The crevasse dropped away, almost dragging me with it. Sheer and white-blue and terrifying. Everything suddenly seemed slow, faraway, unreal. The cold and the shock and the fright seemed to turn into an overwhelming numbness. My brain slugged through treacle as my heart pounded and raced, struggling to process. People don't just walk out of their front doors onto snow swept mountainsides! And yet I teetered on the edge of a crevasse. I could have just leaned forward, ended the dream, but that thread leading back to Jane wouldn't let me give in just yet. Slowly, I backed away.

It took me a while to accept that I just didn't know how to get back. To move the door where I wanted it to go, I mean. To accept that I'd have to appear home by chance, or hope that perhaps over time the pattern would become clear. I copied a map of the world from an Atlas straight onto the wall in the kitchen. On the occasions that I could tell roughly which continent we might be on I added a pin and a number corresponding to my notes on how I had turned the handle. I threaded bits of string between each point to try and map the path. I considered taking a smaller copy of the map out with me to ask locals where we were, to make it more accurate, but decided it was too risky. It would just attract attention.

I set my mind to what had lead me here in the first place, and tried to find out as much as I could about the Sickness. The Collection was a godsend. Not so much through the information it carried (I read a lot about the effects of radiation and didn't find anything that described the symptoms I'd seen) but for the facilities. Somewhere safe and dry to work, with food and sanitation. I only wished I'd been able to bring Jane with me, although I told myself I'd do better than that - when I came home I'd bring a cure. I had the hazmat suits, and the safe that looked thick enough to contain radioactive samples. This in its own right would give me the opportunity to study the Sickness and the radiation which caused it. First, however, I needed a confirmed source.

I took to visiting a new place every day, only stopping longer when I found leads to follow or badly needed supplies. Tia had hoped that whoever came next would travel the world helping people in a much more immediate way. But she hoped a lot of things. How she expected someone to get into the middle of the bloody Himalayas to discover The Collection goodness only knows. Even if someone knew it was there they would be insane to attempt the journey. Helping people directly, like she wanted, was dangerous - they start to suspect you have something they don't and they come after it. I did give some things here and there, but only when the need was dire. Generally I kept to myself and looked for signs of Sickness.

Some days the places I opened onto would be deserted, the doorway simply a square hole in a rock or a long ruined building. Those days I let Rohini out to hunt and sat down to research, trying not to let my mind wander to the panic-inducing thought of being lost. I wished I had a Geiger counter. Tia might have been happy to trust Rohini to growl at the door, but I'd sure have liked something a bit more robust. Still, I wore a hazmat suit every time he growled, just in case. Better safe than Sick.

Reading Tia's notes was interesting. I even paused my research to look up the story of Theseus and Ariadne. At first I thought the common factor in Tia's family contracting the Sickness was Yellow Hat's briefcase. Her father went first. It was then stored in the safe for a while, although I suspect her father had it out of containment on a number of occasions. Both children contracted. The mother may have survived, had she not picked up the briefcase to take it back to 'Yellow Hat'. She ended in stupor like Jane and Mr Jones. Evidence to date indicated that this could be due to a huge concentrated dose of radiation. Instead of going slowly insane and taking their own lives, the victim's mind regressed to protect itself.

Then I saw the flaw in my briefcase theory. If that was the source, why didn't the father suffer that fate? No, it must have been something from the location the briefcase was taken from! The case may have been contaminated but, given the number of regressed minds described near 'Yellow Hat's' residence, I started to suspect the real source of radiation was there. It must have been potent to have affected the population so severely.

I became determined to find that place. To take The Collection there for a third time, go out with the hazmat suit on and find the source. Bring a sample back to study. Perhaps there would be something that could counteract this form of radiation; its effects seemed different to anything documented from before the Cold. But it couldn't be tested without a sample.

It took many months of travelling from place to place to find the shepherd's hut. I could feel the tension building in my chest, the string drawing tighter. For the first time I was almost glad of Jane's state. She would continue her routine, left behind without me. I hoped she wouldn't notice I was gone.

I wasn't sure at first. Rohini didn't growl at the door. Once I was out and looking around, however, the environs were similar enough to Tia's descriptions that I went back for the suit.

It was a hot dry place. A few patches of yellowed grass and twiggy bushes scattered the landscape - the hardy type that survived the Cold but weren't useful for much other than firetwigs. But as I crested the hill to the North I was greeted with a spectacular sight. There, laid out in front of me, were fields. *Green* fields. Impossibly lush. My heart rose for the first time in months. The valley was full of them. Different fields contained varied plants, though I couldn't say I recognised any. Amongst the fields, as Tia had described, moved people carrying water, digging, tending, harvesting. From a distance they looked like a busy community in a healthy world. I stopped for a moment, drinking in the scene in relief. It was almost easy to hope.

But my joy was short lived. The closer I got to the people, the more their movements became familiarly unnatural.

I walked along the dirt track between the crops, watching them go about their work. They were like automatons, just as Jane was when she went about her daily tasks at home. I stopped next to a field where a group were digging the ground over and approached the nearest worker cautiously. None of them even looked up, though my suit made a swishing noise as I walked. Slowly, I laid a hand on the man's shoulder. He did turn at that, gazing blankly in my direction.

"Hello." My first word was too quiet, the suit muffling attempts to communicate. "Hello!" I shouted, but his face remained blank. "What are you doing?" I gestured as well as I could in the bulky suit to emphasise my words.

After a pause the man replied tonelessly. "Digging."

"Why are you digging?" I bellowed through the suit, loud but I hoped not aggressive. No answer. This was familiar. Cautiously, I tried again. "Who told you to dig?"

"Boss."

"What is the Boss's name?"

No answer.

"What is your name?"

No answer.

I smiled to myself.

Having asked a string of questions, like Jane, only the simplest gained a reply. Anything complex or remotely linked to emotion was greeted with a blank stare. The flutter of hope hesitantly flickered back to life. My theory was being confirmed. These people had the same symptoms as Jane. This might actually be leading somewhere. It seemed that something else could also be gleaned from this. Jane only did things as instructed. These people had been ordered to tend the fields. I tried one more tentative question.

"Where does the Boss live?"

A slow hand raised and pointed along the road I had been following. As I moved down the road the man returned unthinkingly to his digging.

It wasn't long before I came upon the cottage. A sudden panic seized me as it came into view and, on instinct, I moved to the edge of the road, crouching low between two fields of tall crops. I was abruptly aware of how bright my orange hazmat suit was.

I took a few deep breaths, air hissing through the tubes, and tried to assess the situation. Here were hundreds, if not thousands, of citizens afflicted by the Sickness and put to work. I reminded myself that I had no reason to assume they had been intentionally exposed to create a workforce, and scolded myself for jumping to sinister conclusions for which I had no evidence. I must just be shaken by the ghostly forms moving around me.

I tried to calm myself by rationally going through the facts. A large number of people had suffered the Sickness, though whether they had contracted it here was not known. It was likely they had been instructed to tend these fields. Whether whoever had instructed them was still present was unknown. However, it was unlikely that anyone would let all this fresh food go to waste.

...Fresh food. Was it? Or would it be so tainted from the very ground that it would be useless? A horrible thought struck me. Useless, unless it could be used to infect others, growing a larger and larger work force until one day in the far distant future the plants had cleansed the soil?

Jumping to conclusions again! Still, I tore a few stems from the plants around me, stuffing them into the pockets of the suit.

What would the reaction of the local Boss be to my intrusion? Would I be seen as a threat? I wasn't sure but, despite the butterflies in my chest, my thoughts were becoming calmer and I wanted to see if I could find any source of radiation. A thing that radiated so strongly it could rob people of their minds. I was getting less and less convinced that I would be able to recognise it, even if I did find it lying somewhere here in the centre of the maze. Perhaps I should have brought Rohini.

I set off towards the house, working my way through the labyrinthine fields of tall crops, and avoiding the road. There were no signs of life, though the tatty wooden door stood open, giving a glimpse of the cool shaded interior beyond. Highlighting how hot and sticky I was in that suit, under the relentless sun.

Five steps and I was inside, in the gentle relief of the shade, but intensely aware of the noise of my own breathing, every tiny rustle of the suit. Whitewashed stone walls lined the hall. Through a doorway to my right I could see the edge of a basic kitchen. I crept around the corner and there it was, on the simple wooden table in the centre of the room – the battered leather briefcase.

I looked around me, having to turn my whole body to see properly. Nobody in sight. I stepped up to the table and pulled the briefcase towards me. The suit's gloves made my hands large and clumsy. I fumbled to get purchase on the catches.

Click.

Click.

Slowly I opened the case…

… it was empty.

I heard a sound behind me and spun round. There in the doorway was Yellow Hat, just as Tia had described him. He was smiling the monstrous smile of someone who takes pleasure in things most people would flinch from.

"Good afternoon, Theseus."

I opened my mouth to reply, but whatever I was going to say slipped away from me like string through my fingers. I searched for it but everything seemed to be unravelling, my busy mind becoming quieter and stiller and emptier… until only one thought remained.

I'm sorry, Ariadne.

ITHAKA

by Felix Pearce

Felix Pearce is a speculative fiction writer living in Cambridge, UK. To date he has had the sort of life that other people describe as colourful and interesting; in his spare time he tries valiantly to prevent it becoming any more so. He enjoys swing dance, costume making and leaving smoking holes in society's concept of normal. He prefers to write happy endings, but the editor made him put in the sad one.

I never meant to stay in one place for so long.

It was in the heat of summer, in Anatolia, that I broke my leg. I came upon a herd of sheep grazing in a sprawl across the hillside path, and was in their midst before I heard the snarls of the two immense dogs that guarded them. They wore iron collars bristling with spikes as long as my hand, and the sheep scattered in bleating panic as they raced towards me. I turned tail, slipped on a loose stone, and tumbled down the steep hillside to fetch up with a sickening crack against an outcrop of rock.

The shepherd found me, drawn from his nearby hut by the commotion. The dogs watched me from a distance, mollified by my pained groans and stillness, but came willingly to his hand when he appeared. He was a taciturn man, as was his equally weathered son, who came that night with fresh food supplies and returned shortly after with a donkey cart to carry me to the village. I lay for weeks in the house of the kenning-woman, but her wizened hands knew their business and my leg healed straight and true. She nodded when I told her of my destination: she too had heard of the kenning-man of the inland sea, a man who kept old things alive, old wisdoms. I had already crossed one sea to get here; she knew that the other sea was to the north, and that the kenning-man lived on the western side of it. I thanked her profusely and remained another week once my leg was sound to fetch and carry for her. But midsummer had come and gone, and I yearned for the road.

I came to the shores of the inland sea as the summer's heat was fading from the air and the mornings were becoming crisp and pale. I looked out on the slate-grey water and shivered; the chill of the nights roused a bitter ache in my leg, and I knew that the winter would be a misery. But I set my jaw, as stubborn as the pain, and turned west to where I hoped knowledge lay.

It was on a day of incredible beauty, a huge and empty sky above me, that I came to the palace.

It was a sumptuous place; or had been. Among the tussocks that spread before it coloured cobblestones lay chaotically slanted, hinting at some pattern they had once been laid out in. Pillars supported a long balcony that swept along the front of the building, a crumbling balustrade above them. Behind the balcony was a vast shell-shaped window, its glass still intact in places, and above that rose a graceful, angular roof. I squinted at the edge of the roof and saw that huge letters adorned part of it: CAZINO. Perhaps that had been the name of the ruler for whom the palace was made. Stepping underneath the balcony, I found a yawning, doorless opening leading inside.

"Hei?" I shouted into the dim interior; the one thing I knew of the local language.

A voice called something back. I waited, and after a few moments I heard footsteps. It was a young man, scarcely as old as I'd been when I left the Isle. He was slender but wiry, sharp-boned and tough. His skin was white, as if he worked indoors. He repeated what he had said in the local tongue, looking mildly annoyed.

"Trade talk?" I asked him. Almost everyone knew a few words of the traders' pidgin.

"Nyet trade," he said, folding his arms. "Nyet buy." He made as if to disappear back into the palace.

"Nyet trade!" I agreed hastily, showing him empty hands. "You talk? Find way?"

"Way from town," he said curtly, pointing down the road to the patchwork of dwellings I had come from.

I shook my head, pointing at the ground. "Nyet find way dom vot. Find way deliquo. Find way book dom."

His expression sharpened. "Book dom?"

I nodded.

He narrowed his eyes for a moment then appeared to come to a decision, beckoned and turned away. I followed him inside the palace, into a tall atrium flanked by a curving stone staircase. He led me up it, avoiding the cracks and missing stairs with the air of long practise. I stumbled after him, only raising my eyes as we came out onto the upper floor. He led me to a doorway, flanked by wooden doors that hung drunkenly off their hinges, and stepped inside.

"Book dom," he said, spreading his hands.

It was a huge, lofty room, the walls covered with fine plaster that bore the ghosts of flowing coloured designs. Shell-shaped panels echoed the great window I had seen from outside. Heaps of debris covered the floor, and I glanced up to see that much of them had come from the ceiling - black mildew stained it, verdant moss spread outwards from one corner, and only fragments of the same gorgeous plasterwork still clung to the bones of the roof. But the grandeur of the place was not what made my heart trip. Everywhere upon the plaster was what looked like a vast swarm of flies. They were letters; words. Carved into the plaster and darkened with charcoal-like ink. I ran to the nearest wall, forcibly restraining myself from reaching out to touch the words, but when I came close to it my heart skipped again, this time in despair. The letters were the ones I knew but the words were not - my beloved letters clumped in alien sequences, like unfamiliar plants. I couldn't read it.

As I looked around, taking in the rickety ladders that stood against the walls and the height to which the letters ran on all of them, I realised something else. I had seen a book in the hearth-hall at home; its pages were thin as dry birch leaves and all of them were densely covered with letters smaller than my fingernail. So many words were crammed into that dainty object - all of these walls, covered though they were to as high as the kenning-man could reach, could not possibly hold more knowledge than that single book. This place was a book-house, but it was not the place I was seeking.

My expression must have given me away.

"Nyet?" asked the young man.

I chewed my lip, trying to express what I meant in the traders' unwieldy jargon. "This place book dom," I said. "One book dom, ajin, da? I find way for boku book dom. Hundred book dom. Book dom ride, go deliquo. Come trade, go deliquo."

He looked from the walls to me. "You find way book dom," he said. It wasn't a question. He understood.

"Yes," I said.

"Da," he replied, nodding vigorously. He seemed excited. "I talk you. I talk all chivyek. Find way. Book dom..." He stopped, and said something in his own language.

"I don't understand."

"Trade chivyek bring vishye, trade vishye. Farmer chivyek bring goat, trade seed. Minya want nyet seed. Minya want book vishye. Book dom... book dom learn make vishye. All vishye. All chivyek nyet see chivyek want, bat all chivyek want book dom."

Everyone needed what the Collection had. They just didn't know they needed it.

The kenning-man had pale, piercing eyes. He was, now that I had a moment to absorb him, quite beautiful.

We came to a sort of unspoken agreement. He showed me the room where his cooking fire smoked and a straw-stuffed cot stood waiting. I rolled out my own blanket and settled in to wait until we could find some hint of the onward road.

Autumn darkened into winter as I waited in Cazino's palace. I gathered wood, mended the ladders when the treads broke, and was sent weekly to the village for food and the fine twigs of charcoal the kenning-man used to keep the letters crisp and dark. I wondered what it was he traded for them to begin with, but after a few days a rabble of children from the village came barrelling in, and I watched, bemused, as he taught them the letters from the wall. They scratched the garbled-looking words in the sand with twigs and pebbles, and he, smiling, gently corrected them. He tried to teach me, but I threw up my hands in despair after a single evening.

"Stra-een," he said to me, laughing.

I had been there two months when I woke in pitch darkness to the kenning-man shaking me violently, shouting something desperate in his own tongue over the sound of a torrential storm. I bolted to my feet and followed him into the book room; lightning flashed, and then I understood. Part of the roof had crumbled and fallen in. Icy rain was pouring in through the gap, smearing down the walls. The demon water crept towards the letters, inch by inch. Frantic, the kenning-man shoved a bundle of something - oilcloth, I realised - into my arms and shoved me towards the staircase, running for one of the ladders.

Outside the raindrops hit me like stones and I gasped. Slipping and stumbling, the kenning-man dragged me to the end of the balcony, jammed the ladder into a corner of the masonry, and began to climb. Silently praying for the fates to lend me the feet of a mountain goat, I followed him.

On the edge of the roof the wind tugged at us, shoving the oilcloth against me and making me stagger. I dropped my weight into a crouch and shuffled after him. He was grabbing loose chunks of stone, looking back at me and shouting, the wind whipping away words I couldn't understand. But it was obvious enough; the gash in the roof was narrow, and slowly we began to weight down the edges of the oilcloth with the stone, unrolling it a few inches at a time lest the wind catch both it and us and dash us to the broken slabs below. I doubted it would hold but the desperation on the kenning-man's face was naked. And I understood. Those smudged letters were a fragment of the same treasure I was searching for.

The next day dawned grey and heavy. The lightning was spent but the sky still poured out a steady, drumming rain. I woke not on my own pallet but crammed into half of the kenning-man's cot; after the rescue we had shivered together into slumber, our dripping clothes slung over poles close to the fire. His place beside me was still warm but he was absent. I shuddered at the notion of donning my still-damp shirt, but dressed and went out into the book room nonetheless.

Light struck down into the chamber from the rent in the roof above. I had been right; the tarpaulin hadn't held. Half of it hung down into the room, streaming water from a corner. All of the wall below it was soaked, dark with moisture. A lonely figure stood stiffly in front of it.

I went to him and looked at the wall over his shoulder. The rain beat down and the corners of the letters wept black tears, oozing toward the ground. The words were blurring, steadily washing away; the plaster, already powdery with age, threatened to crumble into sludge. Even as we watched a gobbet of it fell from the top of the wall. I touched his shoulder; he turned. Tears of frustration stood in the corners of his eyes and I felt for him. Silently, I pulled him against my chest, folding his head under my chin.

"It's all right," I told him softly. "There's a place, somewhere, where all of this is already safe. Dry and warm and out of the weather. I'm looking for it. I'll find it, I promise you. It won't be forgotten."

"Eu nu te înțeleg," he said.

I rested my forehead against his. "It will be all right."

The next day, when the rain had waned, I took some of the sticks of charcoal from our store and brought them to the rain-soaked wall. I began to darken in the shapes I could still discern, those that had not been eroded too badly by the storm. As I did so I realised that these weren't the same as the other letters; they were angular things made up of curves and strokes and crosses. I wondered why there were two ways of writing at all.

After a while I heard his footsteps behind me. I turned and held out a piece of charcoal. He sighed long and deep, then took it and gave me a sad half-smile. I laughed when he reached out and corrected a letter on the top line.

"This is different," I said to him, uselessly. "What does it say?"

But for once he seemed to understand me; he began to read it aloud to me, and I realised it was in a different language to his tongue. It was long and full of sadness; there was music in it, rhythm and assonance, and over and over again he said the same word. Ithaka, Ithaka.

After the end of it he smiled at me again, more genuine now, and began to re-darken the rest of the shapes.

"Ithaka," I murmured, tasting the word.

From that night on we slept beside one another.

Spring came slowly, as loath as I was to venture out into the cold. But come it must; the moist wind began to touch my face with promises. We had had no word of the Collection, and I knew I could no longer wait for it to come to me.

One day, as I stood in the great portico, I felt his hand on my shoulder. The way down the coast was wide and empty, and the sky above it a piercing blue. It pulled at me, whispering of secrets unsought, of waters untapped. Reluctantly, I tore my eyes away from it and looked into his face. His eyes were full of something I couldn't name.

"Ithaka," he said to me gently, and I knew it was permission for me to leave.

Seven weeks later I found the centre of the world. It was long, cylindrical, its sides peppered with twin rows of holes. It lay broken over a sand dune, tangles of nameless blackened things sprouting from within. I sketched it in charcoal on the hearthstone of the house that took me in. The oldest man of the family nodded and drew out a flute, miming playing it and then striking the hearthstone hard, setting his hand between the drawing and the heat of the fire. I understood; it was God's Flute, the terrible instrument he had played, whose music tore open the sky and called down the Cold.

There were no villages close to it and the people stayed away, leaving it to the rain and the sand.

As I travelled east the faces around me grew dark-skinned and their language ever stranger. They spoke the traders' tongue with heavy accents and there were many places where I had to stay for days before I could come to an understanding with the people who knew things. I looked for the farmers who had long wind-powered screws to draw up water for their crops, the smiths who could make metal stronger than iron, the artificers who made fireworks that lit up the sky when the great puja festivals arrived. And they always told me the same thing: she was here, but now she is gone. I've heard of someone a village or two over who learned something from her too, perhaps you should travel a little further and ask again?

And so I travelled.

Mountains rose up before me as if to mark the extent of my hope. The language and the people changed again, this time to faces like those of the northern traders, eyes folded and cheeks smoothed out as if the Cold had worn their features away. I sat in a tiny room drinking a rich, buttery tea; outside, shaven-headed men in saffron robes turned wheels in honour of the sky.

The saffron-clad man who sat opposite me, stout and compact, seemed to come to a conclusion. He stood and beckoned me. Along a narrow stone-flagged path he led me, into a garden so still it was as if the air held its breath. Rocks and pools were carefully arranged, plants spilling around and under them. He tugged me into one very particular spot and said to me in the traders' tongue:

"You will find it."

I stared at the garden for a long, slow time before I left. It was only three days later that I looked up the valley and saw the same shapes as the garden, writ large in the craggy shoulders of a mountain pass.

I had never climbed so high before; the air was thin and the shaggy beasts bearing the trade caravan's goods were sullen. I stopped every so often to look behind me and at last, as we neared the top of the pass, I saw the monk's garden yet again, laid out like a cloth in the valley below.

I turned, casting about for some sign. No paths branched from the main pass trail. Nothing broke the grey monotony of stone except pockets of snow, achingly white in the sunlight. The traders halted, exchanging glances with one another, and grouped up the yaks. Some of them began to share out food while others settled in to a game of dice.

There was a turn in the trail not far ahead of us and beyond it the valley was hidden from view. This was the place the monk had meant me to find, I was certain. Further below the view had not been like the garden, distorted. It should be here. I started to search more carefully.

Under an overhang, sheltered from the wind, was a massive boulder with a smooth, flat face. It was as blank as the rest of the mountain and I dismissed it at first, only to return to its relative warmth as the thin wind chilled me to the bone. I slid down with my back against the rock, baffled and disheartened.

"You find?" asked a trader boy curiously, the rope attached to the halter of his yak all but taut where he'd moved towards me.

"Nyet," I said. "Only zigsa crap." I gestured at the animal scat that lay close by. The boy looked at it, then back to me. I ignored him.

A few moments later a heavier tread came towards me, catching my attention; the boy had brought one of the men back with him. They examined the snow-cat turd closely, as if they were trying to read omens in it. At length the adult turned to me.

"Nyet zigsa," he said firmly. "Too big." He held up his left thumb and finger a moderate distance apart. "Zigsa," he said, then held up the right, almost twice the distance. "This."

I was suddenly alert. The Curator was said to own an immense, lethal cat. "Find!" I beseeched them, scrambling up. "Find all vishye. All help!"

There was shouting and chaos as the whole caravan of traders was roped in to help. Not a pebble in the pass was left undisturbed. It was the boy who yelled in triumph at last, and ran to me with a pale object in his hand. The traders gathered round me, on tenterhooks as I examined it.

It was like the leaves of the book I had seen in my hearth-hall; light, stiff, dry-textured. But it was crumpled, scrunched into a ball that fitted perfectly into my palm. Gingerly I tugged at folds and corners, unfurling it slowly.

It was not covered with tiny, dark letters as the book's fine leaves had been. Instead large, loosely formed ones made of some grey substance ran here and there in places across it. Except for the three words at the top of the page all of the writing was run through with sharp, vicious lines - in some places the tip of whatever instrument had written it had punched through the sheet to the other side. As if the writer had been angry, desperate to record something but unsure how to begin. It took me a moment to piece together the words; the leaf rustled a little in my trembling hand. The first of the crossed-through phrases was my answer.

This is the Collection. It is ho'

I checked the top line to be certain. It said *'Read This First'*. Nothing useful. I looked again at the great flat-faced boulder. It was the perfect size to house a door.

The Collection had been here. But it was gone.

The monks were kind when they realised my situation, and I was humbled by their understanding. I was sitting in the courtyard, the wasteland of despair inside me untouched by the frugal warmth of the mountain sun, when the same monk who had shown me the garden came with steady eyes and beckoned me to follow once again. He led me to a room I had never seen opened before and for the second time that day I almost dropped to my knees, overwhelmed.

It was a Collection.

Devices I could not name stood in corners. A thing shaped like a yak's horn but made of metal, mounted on three spindly legs. A complicated brass instrument, hunched over a plate as if peering at something held in its own grasp. A beautifully made balance, with weights marked not in bullets but with numbers followed by a 'g'. And all around the walls wooden shelf-cases housed actual books.

I gaped, barely remembering to thank him. He only nodded. He went to an alcove near the door and unrolled a long cloth index. I hovered at his shoulder, peering breathlessly, only to see that what was embroidered upon it was yet another language I didn't recognise. I marvelled. How many writings were there in the world?

The monk, ignoring my hiccupping breaths, went to one of the cases and picked a book. He held it out to me.

"You take," he said. "You use. Take to book dom."

I looked at it. The first few letters on the cover spelled BOOK. A book of books? The ground under my feet seemed to tilt. What power had I been granted?

I stayed there until I had examined every volume. Some were in my own tongue, some in others. I found that the mere presence of each one, the existence of this whole place, prompted more questions than ever. Could there be more little-Collections like this one? Others like me, like the kenning-man, searching for what had been lost?

One book was titled in the strange curve-and-angle letters I remembered from the palace wall. My fingers brushed its spine, remembering those letters read aloud in a familiar voice. Remembering Ithaka.

The book I had been offered was a small miracle; the monk had been wise in his selection. I made ready to leave. On my last day there, I went to the little-Collection for the last time to say a fond goodbye. I smiled once again at that drab little cover and picked it up to leaf through it, simply for the warm nostalgia the letters raised in me.

My eyes widened. Inside it were indeed the strange angular symbols I remembered from the ruined wall. But opposite them, on every right-hand page, were blessed familiar ones. Trailing vines of words that ran down only half the page, as if they were trying to reach something far below. I looked at the front for an index, and found that the titles of each word-vine were given in both languages.

And one of them was 'Ithaka'.

Half disbelieving, I turned slowly to the page and read the translation with awe. When I had finished I knew why the kenning-man had let me go.

Ithaka gave you the marvelous journey.
Without her you would not have set out.
She has nothing left to give you now.

And if you find her poor, Ithaka won't have fooled you.
Wise as you will have become, so full of experience
You will have understood by then what these Ithakas mean.

It took me long months to find my way back to Cazino's palace. During the wild, warm storms of late summer I sheltered in an echoing painted cavern along with the people of the nearby villages, and in the dim flickering light of the fire I turned the pages of the gift the monastery had bestowed on me. Clumsily I sounded out words and wondered at the meanings that unfurled.

I passed God's Flute in spring, coneys darting away from the path to the safety of the warren they had dug beneath its side. It had crumbled a little, the orange-brown fingers of decay reaching ever further around its pale body. I wondered how long it would be before it became only a memory, a stain in the sand, the half-forgotten reason why that warren of coneys was too sacred to hunt and eat. I looked up at the sky and could almost see in the distance that piercing shade of blue.

It was summer again when I reached the sea. Insects chirred in the harsh grasses and gulls screamed their derision above my head. I turned west along the coast and the warm sky passed above me, always leading me towards that misty strip of horizon far away.

The palace too had crumbled in winter's hands. One corner of the balcony drooped now into rubble and my heart kicked painfully in my chest; what if he had abandoned it?

But as I drew close I heard the tink-tink-tink of a hammer and I knew he was there. Quietly I picked my way up the staircase, following the sound. He was tapping a stone into place in a roughly made buttress. It and its brother supported a wooden roof that shielded the letters of the Ithaka poem from rain. The gash in the roof had widened, I saw, and now even fewer of his precious words were safe from the sky. More of the wooden roofs stood at intervals around the room.

For long moments I watched him silently. The book hung over the room, ready to fall into his world just as weightily as the roof above my head. In my heart was the knowledge of that other store of letters, but in my hands was the power to show him his work was not in vain. I drew the book out of its wrappings and with a deep happiness I read the familiar words on its cover again: *Bookbinding and Papermaking.*

Deliberately, I knocked a crumb of plaster from a nearby block to the ground. He turned, and at last I saw that cold, piercing sky-blue I had searched for for so long; the omnipotent sky above us, echoed in his eyes. They were wide as they fastened onto the book in my hand.

I spread my hands, gesturing at the ground around me, at this place. His home.

"Ithaka," I said to him.

He smiled.

SHADOWS IN THE LIGHT

by Ed Gray

Ed Gray has been an inveterate dissembler for many years, and finds writing bios quite hard. In his time, he has been a radio technician on helicopters, a coastguard, an audio/ visual maintainer, a father of 3 children, periodic fanfic writer, a LARPer, an astronaut and an occasional liar. Ed is currently an aircraft engineer in Cambridge, UK. He plays far too many video games, and still refuses to eat the mice the cat brings him.

PART ONE

It was a myth, a story, a tale of hope that people huddled in the dark told each other to help them believe that things could improve, even when they clearly wouldn't.

Which meant that the woman Zinaida was watching at the moment couldn't possibly be the Curator. TwoFingers had sworn up and down it was, but everyone knew how reliable Fingers was... that was why he only had two fingers left. Why would someone from a myth come to this hole in the ground?

The stranger was tall for a woman, worn, made broad shouldered and lean by a lifetime of hardship, her clothes as dirty and as torn as everyone around her. Nothing about the way she *looked* made her stand out in any way from the other villagers, her black hair was shot with grey like everyone else's. But the way she walked... that was a different matter. The way she carried herself. This was a woman comfortable with authority, being in charge. She wasn't a merchant and she wasn't a mercenary. She lacked the former's watchful nerves and the latter's menace.

And Mikaelanovitch had let her in, apparently heard her out. That was... odd.

***

"We have something you need."

The vozhak eyed her sceptically over his steaming bowl. "I doubt that, unless you can provide clean water, sunshine, food..?" He snorted at his own cynical humour, shaven head gleaming in the flickering lamplight.

The leader's stone hut was the most solid structure in the village, solid enough to even keep the wind out. It boasted a low table, some half decent furs and hides, and a battered samovar apparently made out of an old artillery shell case.

The stranger shrugged with a low sweep of one of her hands. "Those, no. Short supply these days." She leaned forward, took her own bowl with the other hand. "But we can help you stop everyone here from dying when the Chirkeyskoye Dam gives way."

Mikaelanovitch drank slowly, watching the stranger over the rim of his bowl. Dark almond eyes met his steadily; no challenge but no withdrawal, confident of her offer. He set his bowl down, put both open hands on the table in a deliberate gesture; empty of knives, inviting discussion.

"Tell me."

"That wall, as strong as it once may have been, is starting to crack. When it goes, so will you." The stranger let the words hang for a few seconds and then placed her bowl aside. "We can teach you how to stop that, how to release the water safely. Take the pressure away and the wall can crumble to nothing, it won't matter."

"That knowledge is long lost and you know it, *moshenika*." The big man took his hands off the table, scowled at her, started to unfold from his seated position. "You waste my time."

The stranger's voice hardened, an edge creeping into her words. "No. No, I do not. I am a caretaker of lost things, not a wandering con artist, *vozhak*. We have the information you would need to do this in our possession, right now." She tipped her head back and stared at the village boss standing over her, seemingly unfazed by his size. "Of course you would have to do the work to fix it. This is not some form of magic and nothing is free."

They stared at each other in the low light. He grunted softly in amusement, sat back down. "No, nothing is ever free. What would you want in exchange for such as this?"

***

The stranger had left the vozhak's home earlier today and disappeared for a while. Zinaida wasn't sure if she'd left the town or not. She certainly hadn't gone through the gates, but there were other ways in and out. Zinaida hung around what passed for the main street for most of the afternoon, pretending to run errands, keeping an eye on the boss's hut. TwoFingers said the stranger had been in to see Mikaelanovitch a few times, claimed to have listened from a scurry hole while they talked of a trade.

She still wasn't sure if it had been worth the scraps of food she'd given him for the story.

***

The Curator made her way along the shelves, flushed in The Collection's dry heat after the cold outside. Carefully, deliberately, she took certain books down, checked them, added them to her satchel, or tucked them gently back.

She hoped it was the dam. It wasn't always easy to tell, but the ancient structure above them in the hills had been decaying for years since the Cold fell, and it was the most likely reason they were here. That and the vozhak's wall ornament that she'd spotted over his shoulder while they talked.

Given enough information, like the book she currently held in her hands, given enough time, maybe the people here could come to harness the waters from the dam again in some way. Maybe a mill of some sort... but that would tip the balance. Too much improvement in a small settlement would attract unwelcome attention, usually detrimental, usually violent.

She sighed as she slid the book back onto the shelf. It was always such a fine line.

***

The *khazri* was picking up as the light faded, the chill edge of its breath starting to cut through Zinaida's battered leathers, and the stranger had still not returned. What passed for autumn simply meant a little more cloud, a little less light, and the *khazri* crossed a lot of open land and water before it got to the town. She hunkered down in the lee of Kolya's collapsed shack, nestled down into the rubble and ash that no-one cared enough to clear, and wrapped her hide jacket in on herself.

Why did she even care who this woman was? The Collection was a fantasy, so this lady must be either a very smooth liar, or crazy, or both. She only had TwoFinger's word that she'd said she was the Curator. Wasn't the Curator meant to be a guy? Why was she so interested anyway? Why..?

Because *what if she **was**...?*

***

She watched the village girl quietly from the shadows. She'd spotted her early in the day when they'd stepped out for a break. The villager had turned away a little too fast as she'd looked over and been a little too studied in her nonchalance. The girl may as well have set up a stall.

She could just re-enter the door behind her, reposition it, and avoid confrontation completely. The satchel bumped against her hip, weighted with notes and sketches. As trades went, this was a pretty safe one. No need to take risks. She still had her knives, hung under her armpits in case everything went to hell, but it was *always* better to leave them sheathed.

She turned back to the door.

***

"What do you want?"

Zinaida shrieked in surprise, cold limbs protesting as she sprang out of her makeshift nest, gravel and ash flying away as she flailed. The adrenaline made her slightly giddy as she spun to face the speaker. The stranger was smiling, crouched in the debris just behind where she had been, and that flustered her more than the surprise.

"I… wha… WHY DID YOU DO THAT?!" A flicker of unease. The stranger would have had to have passed through the ruin of the shack to get to where she was. She hadn't made a sound. Zinaida's stomach dropped. "I'm sorry I'm not doing anything I haven't stolen anything and I'm going, ok? Please don't hurt me!"

The smile vanished. "You think I'm going to hurt you?" The older woman stood up and stepped out of the wrecked building, ducking a fragment of the old doorframe that hung loose. "If I was going to hurt you, I wouldn't have wasted time speaking to you." Up close, the stranger was a lot taller than Zinaida, a *lot*, and suddenly *anywhere else* seemed like a good place to be.

"I know you've been watching me, so I'll ask again: what do you *want?*" Not angry, just… impatient?

She met the stranger's eyes. Dark eyes. Such dark eyes, a faint uplift at the corners, like the people of the Steppes. "…I wanted to know who you are…"

A puzzled look. "Who I am? Why? Why would you care?"

"TwoFingers says you're the Curator."

"The Curator..?"

"The one who looks after the Collection."

A moment of silence as the older woman studied her. The *khazri* whipped around them, cold fingers across exposed flesh, dirt scratching on skin in the growing twilight.

"And now why would that be me?"

"TwoFingers says you told Mikaelanovitch that The Collection was willing to trade for that thing on his wall."

The stranger laughed for a second. "TwoFingers seems to say a lot of things. Does he normally lie a lot?"

"Well, yes, sometimes, but he swore this was true…" Nonplussed, she trailed off as the woman chuckled again.

"Look, girl…" She stopped, frowned. "My apologies, what *is* your name?"

"Zinaida"

"Zinaida, I'll be honest. Yes, I'm trading with your vozhak for something I want. No, I'm not this 'Curator' type. The Collection is a fairy story, something we tell children. How could something like that be real? And don't they say Curator's a *man*?"

Zinaida watched the stranger's eyes as she spoke, uncertain if it was all truth, or just part of it. The woman held her look, faintly amused by something that she couldn't work out. "Where are you from, gospazah? Your accent is… different."

"Ah, a way east from here. You won't have heard of it. Nobody has, unless they're from it."

Zinaida managed a smile. "A bit like here, then?"

"A lot like here, yes." The woman raised a eyebrow at her. "Are we done? May I conclude my business?"

She nodded. "I am sorry to have bothered you. Please… do not mention this to the vozhak? He may be angry at me." She shivered in the wind, only partly from the cold. "I do not desire a beating for asking a stranger's name."

The older woman grunted softly to herself. It sounded almost like disgust but could not have been. Who, honestly, would care? "I will say nothing. Our conversation is ours alone. Goodbye, Zinaida." She turned to leave.

Impulsively, Zinaida reached out, touched her arm lightly. "Gospazah. I am sorry, but… what *is* your name?"

The look that crossed the worn face was sad. Maybe even regretful? With a soft sigh, the woman gave her a wistful smile. "My name is Theseus. Goodbye Zinaida."

She left. Zinaida watched her make her way to the stone hut and enter it, before she thought to get out of the wind.

***

Often there would be no trade, just an open sharing of information that people could use. Sometimes things could be rescued or salvaged – there were still caches, even now. Every last fragment was valuable but retrieving them from their resting places was risky, physically and mentally. There were… things that preferred to be left undisturbed in the dark and the Cold. Things she'd never had dreamt of before the war.

Theseus turned the storage unit over in her hands. It had been many, many years since she had seen one of these in use. It had survived surprisingly well, hung as a shiny prestige item on a villager's wall, but connected correctly back into a network it was beyond value. The lack of electricity might be overcome someday, somehow. She'd felt The Collection would had wanted it, had been willing to trade for it, and she hadn't had to risk life, limb and sanity to retrieve it. A good trade.

She dropped it back into her satchel and glanced quickly around the darkened alley. The ramshackle town was mostly deserted now night had fallen. Only the guards on the walls, patrolling in pairs, were still moving around outdoors. Far off in the distance, something uttered guttural screeches in the dark, a sound that made the back of her neck crawl. Frost was starting to form on the ground and walls. She gratefully turned to face the wooden door set in the alley wall, reaching out to grasp the handle. Warmth and light spilled out from another place, far from the windswept town she was in. She stepped quickly through, the light in the dark narrowed to a flicker and was gone.

***

Hidden deep in the darkness opposite, Zinaida clenched a fist in triumph and frustration.

She crossed the ground between her hiding place and the alleyway at a flat out sprint, the fastest she'd ever run, skittering to a halt in front of the old door. She paused for a moment, pulse thundering in her head, screwed up what was left of her courage and raised her hand.

***

Theseus set her bag down, shucked out of her coat and hung it on the worn brass hooks to one side of the door. Yawning, she reached for the door mechanism handle, ready to crank herself and The Collection on to somewhere else to spend the night.

There was a knock.

PART TWO

Theseus had read something, somewhere, in one of the Collection's books, about light not always behaving as it should. She'd been trying to find a way to brighten the thermal lamps that gently lit and heated The Collection's rooms.

Back before the Cold, some pretty smart people carried out a number of experiments that really hadn't come out as expected. Turned out, if you shone a beam of light through a slit, what you got was pattern of lines, light and dark, not a single bright line.

Not, she had to admit, an experiment she would have ever thought of doing. Their conclusion was that light was both one thing and another, all at once. She hadn't entirely understood it at the time.

She understood now.

She wished she didn't.

***

Theseus was strange, Zinaida had decided. Not that anything she'd come across in the last handful of days had been *normal*, exactly, but she seemed… well, *strange*. Distracted. Almost like she was hearing something Zinaida couldn't, which was ridiculous as Zinaida had some of the best hearing in the village. The older woman was friendly enough, though. She hadn't hit her once, or threatened her. She'd even fed her, expected nothing in trade. Shown her something called a "shower" that water fell out of like rain, only hot and clean. Talked to her about words, and books, and how they held knowledge, like in your head but marked down, trapped in the paper.

Very odd.

There was a big hairy creature that Theseus called Rohini, which lurked in the shelves and corridors of The Collection, just out of sight. Zinaida had found some of its hair rubbed off on the corner of a cabinet. It was quite coarse, some of it orange and white in colour, some of it charcoal black. Nothing she'd ever encountered had had fur like this. She couldn't decide if that scared or interested her. She heard its heavy footfalls sometimes, an occasional throaty grunt. She didn't think that was what Theseus was listening to. The woman had said Rohini would come out eventually, he was just getting used to a new person.

They'd been places without moving. That was *deeply* strange. The village she'd grown up in, everyone she knew, gone, far away. Where it had been was a new landscape, places she'd never seen or even heard of. Theseus had talked about the Door, and the handle, and how it moved, and honestly, if Zinaida hadn't seen it, she would have written the woman off as crazy. She'd always thought that part of the story was nonsense.

Equally, she was warm, dry, safe and fed. She could stomach a little crazy for now.

This time The Collection had opened into the top floor of a shattered fort, something Theseus had called a "bunker", a hiding place dug deep in the ground before the Cold. It was kind of like the Collection but it had been dug to hide people, not books, and it didn't travel, and the people hadn't really planned to leave it. This sounded to her like getting trapped in a scurry hole, like when those feral dogs had cornered her a couple of years ago: you were stuck, nowhere to go. She shivered at the thought.

It also appeared that the bunker wasn't maybe as strong as the builders hoped it would be. Something had cracked it open to the sky, torn the very earth itself away from the top of it. She couldn't begin to imagine what that would take. The broken walls were thicker than anything she'd ever seen. Now there were people living in the top level of it like a little town, out of the bitter winds. It wasn't like they'd lost a lot of light, after all.

Where the roof of the bunker had torn away, subsistence crops had been planted in the soil that sifted down from above. The rooms that still had a ceiling were being used as living space. The whole thing was dingy, slightly smoky from the lantern oil the residents were using, and cluttered by the pieces of rubble too big to move and too hard to break.

They'd gone into the heart of it, spoken to a number of people, and always Theseus would ask about what they needed, how they were. Zinaida stayed quiet in her shadow, listening, learning, watchful. Their language was distorted, a twisted version of the Trader's Tongue. Thick accents made it hard to follow some of the exchanges. She watched the people, she watched her colleague, and she saw how their words pulled at Theseus. She saw her torn by wanting to help them all and being unable to do so.

***

It was puzzling. These people didn't want help, not openly. Any two books from the Collection could measurably improve their lives but each time she offered, she was rebuffed. It made no sense. They were not so well off they could refuse all help. She'd seen places in much better shape, had helped rebuild some back in the day. *Long ago, gone now. Keep moving forward.*

Maybe it was a pride issue? They didn't seem prideful, more… cautious. Something was off though. She'd traded with enough people now that she was used to the wariness people had towards strangers, and this wasn't it. Well, it was, but there was an extra element she couldn't quite grasp. The couple she was talking to right now dodged most of her questions. The older woman, presumably the mother, was starting to get impatient with her, and the younger one, barely a teenager, avoided making eye contact with her or Zinaida at all. Like everyone nowadays, they were dirty, worn beyond their years, borderline starving.

"Friend, told you. Told you twice, no help you have will be taken. Got all we need."

She forced herself to stay calm. Getting angry wouldn't help. "Look, you must have someone sick here. I've got some notes, just basic medical stuff…"

The older woman took a step forward, cutting her off with an emphatic gesture, scowling into her face. "Enough! Told you no. Suzerain said no, so no it stays."

"The suzerain?"

Before she could answer, the younger woman finally looked up, tugged at her mother's sleeve. "Reynault is sick."

The older woman's face hardened even more as she shook her arm free. "Elle ne peut pas aider! Le suzerain a dit non!"

Theseus recognised the language with a cold shock. It had been a very long time since she'd heard French spoken.

"Pourquoi ne la laisserez-vous pas essayer?" The girl stamped her foot angrily. "What is the worst she could do, maman? Put him right?"

The older woman slapped her. The sound echoed like a whipcrack in the corridor they stood in; one or two people nearby looked over in dull interest as her voice raised. *"Tu penses que je veux que la lumière noire t'emporte aussi?"*

Her French had grown rusty from lack of use, but something about a *dark light..?* Theseus stepped sideways a little, so she was facing the mother, not quite in front of her daughter, but enough to be in the way. She sensed Zinaida shift out to one side, watchful, poised. She spread her hands, palms up and outwards, placating.

"Madame! ...uh... Je suis desole, um, je veux seulment... aider? Donnez secours? Regarde moi Reynault?"

The mother stared at her. "This might kill all of us."

"Reynault has plague? A disease?"

The woman shook her head dismissively and seemed to come to a decision. "Come and look. It is too late now anyway." She pointed a finger at her daughter. "Justine, go and place some offerings. It might help."

They trailed behind her as she led the short distance to where she lived. The door was frozen open, hinges long lost to rust and decay. A tattered leather hide was hung to keep the drafts out. They pushed through into the stinking, dingy room. Blowing a guttering lantern into more life, the woman raised it, stepped over to a piled bundle of rags in the far corner.

"This is Reynault now."

She set the lantern down nearby and delved into the bundle with both hands, dragging a young boy up out of them by the front of a tattered jersey. His limbs fell limply as she propped him up against the wall. Jaw slack, his head rolled loosely to one side, a faint trickle of drool starting to run down his chin. Brusquely his mother gestured them closer as she stood up, gathered her lantern to hold it overhead as Theseus approached.

"This is how he has been for the last month. Before that, screaming, flailing, weeping. Whispering to himself all the time. "

"Reynault, comment ca va? Je suis Theseus." She squatted down in front of the boy, waved a hand in front of the boy's face. When nothing happened, she glanced up at the boy's mother. "May I touch him?"

She shrugged. "Do as you please. It will make no difference. We will all be like him soon anyway."

Theseus stared at her for a moment, then turned back to Reynault. Reaching out, she lifted the boy's head by the chin. There were scars down the lad's forehead and cheeks, quite fresh, not long healed. Theseus sucked in a sharp breath. The shadows on the boy's face weren't shadows: his eyes were missing.

"What... what happened?"

"He tried to claw his own eyes out." Her matter of fact tone sent chills down Theseus' spine. "When we put bags over his hands, he tried to chew through them. He crushed his own fingers then pushed the splinters through the bags."

"Why?"

"He went where he shouldn't have." The woman's face twisted in sorrow, stark deep lines in the lantern light. "He went where he shouldn't have, and he looked at the *lumière noire*, and it looked at him."

Theseus dropped the boy like she'd been stung, stood and spun sharply to face the older woman. "*WHAT* looked at him?!"

The mother gazed back, and she looked sad. Not sad for her son. Sad for Theseus. "The suzerain. Le Vieux Sombre."

Theseus closed The Collection's door behind them, levered the locking mechanism into place. Zinaida had protested at the abrupt departure, pestered her with questions all the way back, and was now pacing up and down by the foot of the stairs to the Observatory, scowling.

Theseus had brought another bed up to the Observatory for the girl. Tia's bed sat, still made, where she'd moved it over to one side. It felt wrong to give Zinaida that bed. Just... *no*.

Zinaida hadn't understood the words, thankfully, but even thinking about them turned her stomach. These people, they needed help she could give. She could maybe even help them to leave, give them the knowledge to survive, to escape.

But to do so would draw its attention. Maybe they should just go?

"HEY! Don't ignore me!"

She came back to herself at Zinaida's shout. The girl was in front of her, furious. "I'm sorry. I promise I wasn't ignoring you."

"Then what, *mudak*? What were you thinking? Why did we run away?" Zinaida pointed at the door, glowered at her from lowered brows. "They're still no better off. Wasn't that why you said we do this, to leave people better off?"

Theseus forced herself to look at her, to look her in the eyes. Like many young adults now, Zinaida was functionally illiterate. She hadn't read The Journal or any of the books Tia had marked, she didn't know, and she hadn't got to telling her all of it, not yet. The girl was still coming to grips with hot water for washing, a door that moved despite being attached to a building, and an animal you kept for friendship not food.

She didn't know about the Dark Ones.

"Look, you know how I said that there are some things out there that we need to avoid at all costs?" Some of the books on Class Eight had little slips of red paper sticking up out of their spines. They had been an education in fear, especially for someone who considered themselves a rationalist.

Zinaida glared. "Some guy living deeper in the hole?"

"IT'S NOT A MAN!" She swore loudly in her own language. Zinaida stepped back, hand dropping to her knife. Theseus blew out an angry breath, paused, inhaled. "It's something we don't ever want to meet. Ever."

Zinaida was silent for a second, thinking. "Like the Shriekers? No-one stays out after dark unless they're a guard."

That is not dead which can eternal lie. The line crossed Theseus' mind unbidden, and she shivered, hard enough that Zinaida noticed. "Worse."

"Worse... Then what do we do?"

Theseus spread the diagram of the portable shelter out across the reading area's tracing table, turned the lantern up underneath it. "I need you to copy this, exactly as you see it."

Zinaida stared at her like she had asked her to flap her arms and fly. "How?"

She gestured at the pot of pencils, the roll of thin paper. "You lay that over the top, then trace out the lines with the pencil..." She trailed off as Zinaida continued to stare at her. "What?"

"What is 'trace'? How can I see it if I put this over the top of it? And what is a pencil?"

"Um... like a piece of charcoal. You follow the lines with it." She laid the tracing paper over the diagram, demonstrated with a few strokes. Zinaida came close, fascinated by being able to see through the paper. "Don't press too hard though or you'll tear it."

"The light does this? Makes the lines show?"

Later on, Theseus would remember her words.

The package wasn't enough, not nearly enough, but she couldn't just leave without leaving something. Couldn't.

You help whoever needs it, no matter what.

With shaking hands, she unwrapped the shotgun from its oilskin, worked the action, once, twice, then loaded it. At close range, this was the most potent weapon she'd got. There were a couple of other choices, but she wasn't as confident with them and her knives weren't enough.

No matter what.

She slung her satchel and then the gun over her shoulders. "Zinaida."

***

The note in Theseus' voice told Zinaida she was afraid. Zinaida had seen and heard fear in people before, it was a fact of life. You got used to it to a degree. The look of sheer terror on Theseus' face had made Zinaida feel hollow, so she'd gone hunting for a weapon while Theseus feverishly copied out notes. The short sword she'd found in a display case was a comforting weight in her hand. It countered the fear a little.

"Yes?"

"I've shown you how the door works. I've shown you where The Journal is. You know where the books that will teach you to read are. If I don't come back, you just go. Take The Collection, take Rohini, and go. Do you understand?" She grasped the girl's shoulders, grip tight with her urgency.

Zinaida reached up with her empty hand and squeezed the woman's arm. "We will both return, but yes. I understand."

The door swung open and she followed Theseus through.

***

The area outside was deserted. They both stood for a second, tight with tension, then made their way back towards the heart of the town. If she could get the drawings to Justine then maybe the young woman would have a chance.

It was waiting. Of course it had known. *Nothing* passed into its dominion without its consent. Every single person they had spoken to that day was gathered before it, all the others to one side, mute witnesses to what was to happen. Justine and her mother were there at the front; the old woman's look was of resignation, Justine's full of fear.

Dark cold light roiled around it, bright but not dazzling, with a sense of sickening wrongness that grew the more Theseus looked at it. She tore her eyes away, and remembered the light experiment, the light that was one thing and another, understood in a way that made her feel ill to her core.

In the periphery of her vision something moved at the heart of the light. Something spoke. It must have. There were words. Their basic meaning was clear enough, but the shadows of these words, they scratched at her mind, whispered of things she could not grasp. Things she could not grasp but feared nonetheless.

*_mine_ _only_ _no others_*

A thud to her left as the sword slipped from slack fingers.

_go_ _continue_
stay _end_

Something wet and sticky began to run from her eyes, her nose. The dark light pulsed, grew. It shone, tearing its way into this reality from somewhere soul-crushingly distant and cold. The people grouped before it began to shine too, lit from behind by this stygian glow.

The light. It made the lines show.

She had a handful of Zinaida's jacket.

The words itched, rustled, tore.

_**go**_

Cold midnight flame engulfed the satchel. It burned her as she tore it loose.

Their silhouettes before her, shadows cast in shadows cast by light that wasn't.

Voices, human voices, raised in discordant... song..? far behind. She threw up, kept moving.

The handle turned. And turned and turned and turned again.

PART THREE

She'd been working in Vietnam when war broke out. As news spread, more and more of the workers, including her translator, abandoned the construction site and the foreign contractor. Alone, scared, a long way from home, she'd sat in her rented 4x4 in disbelief as godlike flashes of light flickered on the horizons, as the airwaves slowly filled with static. Hunger prodded her into action; she dried her eyes and started taking stock. At least she hadn't been in Hanoi. Or London.

Years ago, Tu Thi Linh had become Mrs Linh Paudel and they had honeymooned in Nepal, his birthplace. Struck by its charm, the removal from the pressures of Western life, surrounded by the perpetual peaks of the Himalayas, they'd joked about retreating to Kathmandu should the end of the world ever come about.

If he'd made it out of London in time, that was where she knew he'd be.

***

Something scratchy and wet rubbed at her face, like a damp piece of sandpaper. It was borderline painful; she tried to open her eyes to see what it was, discovered they were gummed shut by something. Flailing, she bumped her arms on large, solid, and furry.

"'s'okay...Ro, I'm awake. Awake! Stop it!" Trying to shove the tiger away was like trying to push over a wall with her mind. She tucked her head into the crook of her arm to stop the tongue bath she was getting, and scrubbed hard at her eyes with the other hand. Rohini licked the top of her head instead. "Dammit, seriously? Gerroff!"

The big Bengal chuffed and started licking her ear as she squirmed.

She managed to crack one eye open. Flakes of dried blood fell away as she rubbed at the other, managing to get it open. Now able to see, she scrambled out from under the cat's affection, using a handful of Rohini's scruff to help haul herself up, and leaned heavily on the tiger. Rohini butted her gently in the hip with her head, nearly knocking her over again.

"Enough, furball!" She tousled the big cat's ears. "It's good to see you too."

Face tingling, head pounding, she looked around. They were below the Observatory, just short of the stairway up to the mezzanine. Overhead, a savage blizzard was driving snow across the glass. The panes were so thick that they reduced the sound to a very faint hiss, almost like tinnitus.

The door, thankfully, was closed.

Zinaida was sprawled face down several feet away, a small pool of dried blood under her head. Theseus couldn't tell from where she was whether the girl was breathing or not.

"Come on, you." She tugged at the tiger's scruff and staggered over towards the prone body, using him as a walking aid. Halfway across she became aware that she'd got vomit crusted down the front of her, and she'd definitely soiled herself. As she collapsed down next to Zinaida, it was pretty obvious the girl had too.

She brushed hair away from Zinaida's face, wriggled a little closer, and was rewarded with the sound of ragged breathing. Theseus shook her shoulder, winced as the burns on her hand flexed and split.

"Zinaida. Wake up. We're… home." *Home. Yes, this was home now.* Nothing. No response. She searched her scrambled memory for the right words. "Vstavay! My doma!"

The girl stirred, groaned, swore softly in her own tongue. Theseus persisted, shook her again. She started awake with a jump, her face coming off the metal floor with a moist sucking sound as she pulled clear of the blood.

"Theseus? Is that you…? …I… I can't see!" She rubbed at her eyes, face streaked with dried blood. "NO! NOT LIKE HIM! *I WON'T BE LIKE HIM!*" Her movements became harder, stronger, panic creeping in.

Theseus shuffled over, grabbed her wrists. "Woah, sshhhh, it's ok, it's just bl… stuff in your eyes, it'll rub out. Easy now."

"*I CAN'T BE BLIND!*"

The words were a shriek, Zinaida fighting to get a hand back her face. Theseus let her, but kept hold of her wrist. She told herself it was in case the girl started to claw at her face again, but the human contact was immensely comforting. Zinaida ground a finger along her eyelid, dislodging some of the crusted blood. There was a sigh of relief as she got an eye open. Theseus reluctantly let her wrists go so she could clean the other side.

The girl looked up and started screaming. She drove herself away from Theseus with thrashing, panicky motions until she hit the wall with an audible crack. Theseus felt Rohini vanish from beside her, bounding back into the safety of The Collection with a snarl. Zinaida's screams tapered off into terrified whimpers as she fumbled for the knife on her belt, eyes not leaving Theseus' face.

"Not like that, not like them…"

Theseus watched for a second, stunned into immobility by the girl's reaction. "…the hell?!"

The knife came free, came up between them, pointed straight at her. "STAY AWAY! DON'T TOUCH ME!"

"Zinaida, what's the matter?" Theseus pushed herself up onto her knees, body aching, hands falling to her sides in exhaustion.

Zinaida kicked herself away again, starting to shuffle along the wall. "What did they do to you?! WHAT DID THEY DO?!"

"What?"

Bewildered, Theseus stared at the girl's blood-stained, vomit-crusted face. Zinaida's bloodshot eyes were wide in fear and Theseus realised how she must look in turn. Blood-smeared, filthy, eyes like burning coals, demonic.

She laughed. It was all she had left in her. The more she laughed, the easier it got, until she was crying with laughter, sore muscles aching as the hysterics swept through. Struggling for breath, she toppled over onto her side, chuckling giving way to sobs as Zinaida stared at her in aghast confusion.

✳✳✳

Linh had taken as much diesel from the construction site as she could find containers for, and searched the area for anything she could find that she could barter with later, including a mismatched pair of knives she'd found in a carpenter's abandoned toolbox, one small and sharp, the other broad and heavy. The small one went in her jacket pocket, the bigger one on the passenger seat. She left the site before night fell, mildly surprised by the lack of traffic. It seemed like, at least for now, people were waiting to see what happened next.

She made good time that night, and the following day. In the evening, as she settled down to sleep in the passenger seat, there was a staccato rattle on the vehicle's roof. Bought on early by the bombs, the first drops of the autumn monsoons started to fall.

✳✳✳

Zinaida sat in the bottom of the shower, knees drawn up, head down, water pouring over her shoulders. The impact across the back of her neck was soothing, and watching the blood swill away was weirdly pleasing. It helped her feel like nothing was wrong.

Which was a lie, of course. Every time she had tried to turn the water off, the whispers started again. The little flickering movements in the shadows came back. The running water kept them away, the sound drowned them out.

She wondered if Theseus could see them too.

***

"She's not well, you know."

I know.

"I don't know what to do. I'm afraid she'll do something… foolish. Do we have any medicine stashed anywhere that would help?

You already know that we don't. Maybe one of the psychology textbooks?

"They're hard work. I swear the authors invented words just to make themselves seem smarter." Theseus sighed and started hanging the wet leathers up around the planting area. She'd peeled the clothes off both of them in the shower, given them a scrub, washed herself. The leather would dry out quickly in the heat; she'd need to remember to oil them before they were next worn. "You know, I don't think she can hear you. Is there any way you could talk to her, reassure her that it'll be ok?"

I'm really sorry, The Collection replied, *but I don't think so.*

***

It took Linh nearly two years, two brutal, heartbreaking years to make it to Kathmandu. As countries collapsed in on themselves, as the temperatures plummeted, people either banded together or turned on each other. In the first week of travel she found her first rape victims, beaten and left to die at the side of the road. After that she wore her knives openly, used them when needed. She stopped only as required, moving on before people got ideas about the lone foreign woman, finding secluded places off the road to sleep. She stole when she had to, ran when she had to, cropped her hair short, bound her chest and wore baggy clothes to hide her figure. When asked, she was merely Paudel, a neutral name that didn't stand out.

The world changed and she changed with it.

***

"Hey, Zin..?" Theseus rapped on the bathroom's doorframe. The water was still running. "You need to come out before you shrivel up." She waited a moment, then stuck her head into the shower room, not quite sure what she was going to see, a little afraid of what she *might* see. She'd fixed the light fitting but she'd cried while she'd done so.

The girl was on her hands and knees, naked backside in the air, trying to look under one of the cabinets. She didn't look up, just continued staring at the small gap at the base.

"Theseus? Get a knife. I think I saw where it went this time."

The older woman paused, frowned, and then went for the knives.

***

Paudel spent her first deep winter with some local farmers in Burma, a family of mostly older people. In some ways they'd been affected the least, their way of life almost unchanged in the last century. They fed her and she taught them how to insulate against the snow, shore up the roofs and walls to take the weight of it, something the lowlands had never experienced before. When the temperatures rose back above freezing a few months later, she took it as spring and set out again. There would be times in the future when she would deeply regret doing so.

***

The thing was still under there, Zinaida was sure of it. She'd seen it out of the corner of her eye, seen the brief flicker of shadow disappear under the cabinet. She felt Theseus step over her as the woman avoided breaking her line of sight, took the long knife as it was pressed into her hand.

"You watch that side." Zinaida slashed hard through the space beneath the cabinet, the knife jolting in her hand as it bit into something. "Got you!"

She pulled the knife gently back, dragging it all out into the light. The blade was embedded in a balled up pair of white gloves. They were immaculately clean.

Distracted by the oddity of it, she completely missed the look of horror on Theseus' face.

***

The passage through Northern India had been the stuff of nightmares. By the time she came across an enclave of people near Siliguri that didn't seem inclined to kill, eat or rape her, she was starving, ragged, numb inside from what she'd seen and had done. Paudel spent the winter there, trading her skills for food, helping to build more shelters. This time the winter was even longer, colder. The world was cooling and it took longer for the spring to come around, such as it was.

They knew she'd wanted to leave, to move on. They'd managed to skirmish up some fuel and a vehicle. She'd stood there, speechless at the gesture, reminded that despite everything, people still had the capacity to be kind. She'd wept for the first time in over a year.

***

The gloves went in the biomass incinerator in the garden area. Theseus scraped them off the end of the blade with a stick, determined not to touch them. She stayed to watch them burn as Zinaida went to find dry clothes for them both. To her immense relief, the gloves had burnt to ash.

"Tia said he'd been here. I'd thought…" She sighed. "I don't know what I'd thought. That we were safe, somehow?"

You're safer than you were.

"Yeah, you say that. If he can just breeze in and out, we're not safe."

He won't come back without reason.

She ran her hands back through her hair, thinking. "You're right about that, at least. She did say it was because they'd pissed him off. I just hope our French friend doesn't have the same abilities."

I think they are completely different entities. I doubt this one will chase you.

"I hope you're right. It's really good to be able to talk to you finally, you know? I've felt you were there all along, but I couldn't hear you."

She turned away from the glowing embers to see Zinaida, a bundle of clothes under one arm, knife ready in her other hand, warily watching her from a safe distance.

***

Actually being able to lash out at something, even a rolled up pair of gloves, left her feeling a lot better. Back in control. When they shut the shower off most of the whispers died back; now it just sounded like it did after someone had shouted in your ear. Zinaida knew she could ignore that. She picked up her own knife again.

That didn't stop her from keeping an eye out as she found clean clothes. For the first time, she was glad for the bland low light that filled The Collection: it didn't flicker, and the shadows didn't move as she passed them.

Back in the basement, she caught the sound of Theseus' voice as she left the lift, clearly in conversation with someone. Someone she couldn't hear. Years of ingrained caution made Zinaida creep to the edge of the garden, where she listened until the older woman turned, broke off.

"Who were you talking to?"

For the first time since Zinaida had met her, the older woman looked uncertain. "I… I don't know if you're going to understand…"

Zinaida felt a flush of anger go through her as the whispers in her ears got louder. She dropped the clothes and advanced, knife coming up. "You're talking to one of *Them*, aren't you? Selling me out to save yourself?"

Theseus' face went blank as she shifted her weight. "No! I wa-"

The whispers become a roar. Zinaida lashed out, quick and low.

She missed. Strong hands gripped her wrists, spun her. Her shins hit the edge of a vegetable bed and she went crashing face first into the mud. Her weapon skittered away. Her arm went up behind her as Theseus' weight drove the wind out of her. Zinaida struggled for a second but only managed to get more dirt in her face and mouth. Remorseless pressure on her arm and back held her in place. Despite it, Theseus' voice behind her was perfectly level.

"You silly bitch. I was talking to The Collection."

***

The mountain road to Kathmandu had still been snow bound. She wasn't entirely sure anymore, but Paudel thought it might now be June or July. Regardless, it was a treacherous, terrifying drive, and subsequent climb into the mountains. The outskirts were guarded, barricades and patrols set up. They greeted her warily. She was the first refugee in months to have made it, and raiders from other parts of the valley still caused occasional trouble.

The guards guided her to the Singha Durbar, formerly home to the Ministries and now the defacto administration building. When the on-duty clerk asked her full name, she stared blankly at him for a minute, desperately trying to remember who she'd been a lifetime ago.

They had a hall set aside for refugees and residents trying to find someone. On its walls were thousands of slips of paper, photographs, pictures. They got newer and whiter the further she went from the door; she added her own name and message to the end of the paper trail, and then started going back through them. She had to know.

It took her four days.

He wasn't there.

She tried to mourn but discovered that somewhere along the way she had lost the ability. To her discomfort, most of what she felt was just an absence of feeling. Maybe she had known all along.

***

It was nice to know her reflexes were still ok, Theseus mused. It'd been a while since she'd had to do that. Now she needed to decide how to deal with Zinaida. The girl had mostly stopped struggling, but was clearly still tense and willing to fight.

You could just throttle her now.

Theseus caught her breath.

It's not as if you've never done it before. It would solve the problem.

She caught herself looking at the back of the girl's neck. Shook her head silently. That was not her way anymore, not now. She'd done what she'd had to, and left it in the past where it belonged.

She's a risk to us now. If she's lost her mind, what happens next time you argue? If you die, what happens to all of this? To me?

Theseus felt her blood rush for a second. It was a fair point. The work had to continue.

If you don't kill her, she might kill you instead.

She'd survived this long by being able to make hard decisions. This was no different.

She reached out.

***

Zinaida felt the older woman's body move, then settle on top of her, felt Theseus's arm go around her neck. She started to struggle. It was futile. Through the rush of panic, the fight for breath, she dimly heard the woman's voice close to her ear.

"You *ever* raise a knife to me again and I will end you. Don't think for a second that I can't or that I won't."

The pressure around her neck and on her back was suddenly gone. Zinaida lay in the dirt, gasping, as footsteps receded into the distance. She heard the lift rattle, counterweights clattering as it ascended.

***

On discovering her skills, the administration put her in touch with the city's construction committee, people tasked with repairing and restoring what had been lost. That... that she could do. As the years began to pass, Paudel tried to help save what they could, improve what they had. Electricity was a fading memory, fuel stocks depleted, so everything had to be done by hand. The city library became their most valuable asset and new books more precious than gold. From time to time, there'd be rumours of a collection, built by some crazy philanthropist somewhere north of Kathmandu. People were in it, she'd heard, helping others out. As fairy stories went, she used to think it was one of the better ones. Occasionally the story came with an embellishment, a young girl that walked with a tiger, the Collection's guardian, the Curator's Cat. She'd laughed, discounted it completely at that point, until she came across the old newspaper cutting, many years later.

She'd been searching the archives at an abandoned shipping company for something else when she realised that they'd shipped a vast amount of cargo and materials north just before the war. Someone had tucked a newspaper clipping in with the invoices, a clipping that talked about a collection of books and art buried into a local mountain for safe keeping, funded by a foreign millionaire, Isaac Leibowitz.

Paudel stared at it in utter disbelief, then grabbed the invoices.

They'd all gone to the same place. A village called Shikharbesi, three days walk away.

***

She cleaned herself up a little and considered hiding in a dark corner somewhere. But the basement was a little too quiet, a little too empty, despite the plants and the clutter. It was too easy to hear the echoes of faint whispers.

Better to face Theseus now, even if she had gone crazy.

Zinaida came out of the lift onto Class 0. Two chairs sat in the middle of the open space. Theseus was in one, dressed now, shotgun sat across her lap. The other chair was a good fifteen feet away. Theseus left the gun in her lap and pointed at the chair.

"Sit down."

She tried to read the woman's face and couldn't. Dark eyes watched her cross the room, watched her sit, gave nothing away. They stared at each in other in silence for a few moments.

"Do you want to tell me what that was about?" Theseus' voice was calm, conversational.

Zinaida wondered for a second when the explosion of rage would follow. She hunted for the right words. "I... I came down and you were talking to someone. Someone that wasn't there."

Theseus made a noncommittal sound, gestured for her to carry on.

"I kept hearing things, like in that bunker... and I thought that meant it was here. And you were talking to it." She paused, looked away. "I keep hearing them."

"Even now?"

She concentrated for a second, listened. "Faintly. They're quieter with you here." She looked up again, met the dark eyes. "Who were you talking to?"

"I told you. I was talking to The Collection." Theseus rubbed her face wearily, sat back in her chair and blew out a long sigh. "I started hearing it properly just after we got back, although now you say you're hearing things too, I've got to wonder if we're both going a little mad."

"I can't hear it."

"No, it said you couldn't." Theseus tipped her head to one side and gave Zinaida a considering look. "The Collection thought I should have killed you downstairs. You just tried to stab me, after all."

A rush of fear; suddenly she felt cold and sick, very aware of the gun in Theseus' lap. "I'm… I'm sorry. I shouldn't have." Tears suddenly pricked at her eyes, confusion welling up in her. "I got scared and the noises got really loud and I didn't think, I did it."

For the first time in years, completely baffled by everything and how she was feeling, Zinaida burst into tears.

***

Shikharbesi was snuggled in between two ridges, just below the permanent snowline. She felt a little silly, asking about a girl with a tiger, right up until the old man she was talking to smiled broadly. Tia? Yes, she'd been here, although not much recently. They had wondered if she was alright up in the mountain. They hadn't seen her parents for a while.

Anticipation flooded her, a choking sensation of having something incredible within reach. She offered to check, casually asked for directions. He pointed up at the nearest peak and told her to follow the path.

***

Theseus let the girl weep. It gave her a chance to think. If Zinaida was hearing noises, then there was a good chance that the voice of The Collection was just her own psychosis showing.

I'm not a psychosis. It actually sounded irritated.

"Yes, but then you would say that." she muttered softly. "How does a crazy person tell if they're crazy?"

Psychological textbooks in Class 1?

She smothered a laugh. At least her psyche had a sense of humour. Unlike Zinaida's. She sobered quickly. The gun was heavy in her lap. She didn't want that to be the decision, but had to be ready in case.

There were a couple of choices. Zinaida had, up until now, been a good person to have around. She learned fast and was useful when they conducted trades. And, Theseus had to acknowledge, it was good to have the company. Good, also, to have someone who could take over if she couldn't carry on.

Come on, be honest with yourself. Someone here in case you die.

"Please shut up for a minute, will you? Do you want me to leave you in the hands of a potential book burner?" She subvocalised her response, not wanting to spook Zinaida more.

The voice fell silent.

On the other hand, if Zinaida was genuinely going over the edge, she might lash out in another murderous fit. That wouldn't just kill her, it risked The Collection ceasing to be of use to anyone. When she'd come here, when she'd found Tia's journal still open on the table beneath the Observatory, she'd realised she couldn't take it back to Kathmandu. The city was surviving, already had its own resources. There were other people out there who didn't, who *needed* the help. The Collection could reach them. It was probably the only thing that could.

It's not up to you, either. You help whoever needs it, no matter what. We're too good at forgetting we're all in this mess together. You have to be above that. Otherwise…
You have to look after them both, Theseus. Please. Please love them both for me.
You have to be above that.

Shit.
Theseus set the safety on the shotgun and put it down. Since the first bomb dropped, life had been one long run of risks. There was a risk she was going crazy too. She didn't know what it would mean if she was, but *no matter what*, she was going to try and help people until she couldn't anymore. At least her kind of crazy seemed mostly benign.
"Zinaida!" The girl looked up, slightly fearfully, eyes puffy and red. "We might be going crazy. We're probably going crazy. That thing has quite likely damaged us both. I don't know how much, yet." Zinaida flinched slightly, involuntarily, as Theseus stood. Theseus showed her empty palms, slowly moved closer, and offered a hand. "But you know what? We've got work to do, and I don't think I can do it on my own."

***

The blizzard caught her almost unaware. Blinded and numb from the cold, Paudel struggled onwards, knowing she was too far from the village to turn back. She slipped, fell, cursed herself for having been so gullible. How stupid to believe she could find a hidden door to a hidden bunker in the vast entirety of the mountains.
Something moved ahead of her. A flash of orange. A high viz vest? After all this time? She shouted, screamed, clawed her way back to her feet and stumbled forward, driven by a burst of hope. There was another flash of orange to her right. She shambled towards it and fell into the cave that had been hidden by the driving snow. Panting for breath, skin burning in the absence of wind, she looked up just in time to see the tiger disappear into the back of the cave. Paudel got back up, mindful of the risks but also of the stories of the Curator's Cat, and cautiously followed.
Deeper into the cave, the light and the temperature started to rise. She found the tiger outside a doorway, the metal door held open with a chair. The big cat looked at her, and then disappeared inside with a flick of its tail.

She stepped through the door after it, out of her world for the last time.
Linh Paudel's journey was finally over.
Theseus' was just beginning.

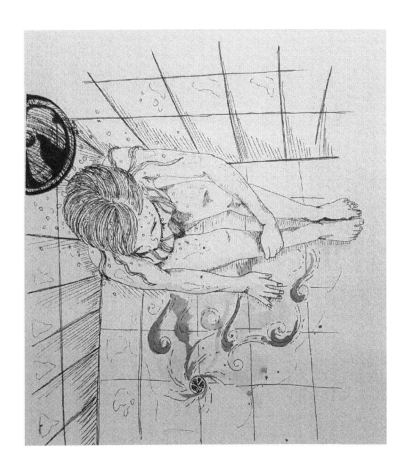

STOWAWAY

by A.A. Thompson

Avid reader and passionate language champion, A.A.Thompson is an English teacher, cat adopter, and daydreamer, who enjoys walking, writing, inhabiting her rich inner world, and spending time with her charming offspring and patient partner. She is particularly fond of the fantasy genre and often takes inspiration from the natural world.

Something wonderful. Impossible, I think, but wonderful.

But I shouldn't start with that. I should start at the beginning, go on to the end, then…. well, maybe not stop, not now.

The beginning... No, it doesn't work chronologically. You'll just have to follow me. I'll tell it as best I can. Whoever you turn out to be.

They, the woman Theseus, and the girl, still haven't noticed me. It's a vast place anyway. Like Tia wrote, you need a ball of string to avoid getting lost. I knew when I read her notes that they weren't really for me. I didn't feel I was the Theseus she wrote for. I was a stowaway, an interloper.

I took shelter in the 800s initially. Hardly anyone went there, even when Tia and Sanna were still alive. It suited me though. I sometimes wonder if The Collection leads you where you need to be.

Sanna was my friend. She was the reason I came. I hadn't seen her for such a long time and when I recognised the door I just slipped in, expecting an excited reunion. Fate has a cruel sense of humour.

There was something far too intimate in seeing her like that. The bulging grotesque twisted mask superimposed on the face of my friend, as she hung limp and beyond all hope. I couldn't move, couldn't speak or scream or react in any way. I was completely absent from the scene I was witnessing; as though I was gazing out through a bubble of glass which protected me from this unreal image. I walked away on legs made of cotton wool and drifted ghostlike upwards into the dome. I recall passing Tia as she slept and wishing she would never wake to see her sister. I wonder now if she heard me, if some small noise I made alerted her to her sister's absence. Ironic how we constantly sabotage our own wishes.

I think it was shame, or guilt, or both, which stopped me from revealing myself. I couldn't let her know I'd seen Sanna first. It felt as though I had robbed her, an unforgivable intrusion to have been there first, to have known before she did. I hid myself until I could work out how to tell her, what to say.

That's how I found the hidden collection. I give it a small c because there is something small and secretive about it, curled away like a magical place from a children's' book. Which is perfect, because that is exactly what it contains. At the back of the 800s when you roll across the central shelving unit there is a small door, a whimsical replica of the Door, with beautiful intricate cogs and wheels like the real door, but it always opens in the same place on both sides. Nonetheless Liebowitz went to the effort of creating this perfect looking facsimile to lead through to Children's Literature, and engraved above it the legend "invenies speranza voi ch'intrate", which took me a while to work out. But I've had plenty of time, and I think, finally, it may have just happened. I will get to that, I promise, but there is more to tell first.

I never did work it out, what to say to her, I haven't used my voice in so long that I'm almost scared to. In fact, I don't think I've spoken a single word since I first slipped through the door looking for Sanna.

After Tia was gone, I waited. I thought maybe when Theseus arrived I could help. I imagined that I would greet his or her arrival, direct them to Tia's notes, settle them in, become their assistant and help them carry on the work of The Collection. So I waited, and I looked after Rohini just as Rohini had looked after me. I've never understood why, even before Tia went, the tiger chose not to reveal my presence, but I suppose tigers have secrets too. In fact, now I know they do. I just need to decide if it will be a betrayal to try to find out more.

I'll be honest. It wasn't at all how I'd imagined, when Theseus arrived. Firstly I thought it would only be a matter of weeks, maybe a month. Tia's note seemed so certain, made the arrival sound imminent. I counted thirteen full moons. She came with a hunter's moon huge and bloody. She exuded something intangible yet recognisable. From the first moment I saw her I could sense death. She was a killer.

I didn't like her, I didn't trust her, and I certainly wasn't going to reveal myself to her.

She took on the duty. Mostly. The practicalities anyway. At least she respected the need for The Collection and she went to help people, taking them the knowledge they needed. I can grudgingly admit she had a skill for that.

She didn't do much for Rohini though. She didn't love Rohini like Tia had. In fact I didn't believe she knew how to love anything, and that validated my decision. I didn't need to reveal myself to her. She could be the Theseus who carried on the work of building The Collection and taking the knowledge where it was needed. I would have a different role. I would fulfil Tia's last wish. So I left her to her business.

The help I took out into the Cold was like the little door to my secret hideaway, something whimsical and a little magical. Its contents were what I took, without ever removing them - the stories which I transformed into puppet shows. I traded a few moments of escapism for whatever people would give, then used my proceeds to trade again for the things I needed to create my terrariums. I grew microcosms, tiny worlds of herbs, propagated from seeds from the catalogue. Then I went back and showed the worried mother of the sickly child, or the anxious husband of the ailing woman, or the desperate son of the fever-stricken father how to sustain the life of the plants and use them to keep their loved ones. This was my way of making it up to her. Even though she never knew my transgression, I felt that if I could use my love of The Collection to spread hope then I would be loving all of them for Tia, and for Sanna too.

That's been my life since I decided to stop being just a stowaway and make myself useful. But I'm getting further and further from the point. It's all intertwined though. I wouldn't have heard stories about Leibowitz if I hadn't gone out with my puppet show, wouldn't have heard bits of the mythology surrounding The Collection which eventually led me into 500 then 530, then 539 until I was trying to stretch my brain around quantum theory, and ideas about multiple universes, because it seemed to be the only thing that made sense if the myths weren't myths after all.

Something has to make sense, because what happened this morning is wonderful. It is also completely impossible unless we don't know everything there is to know about the universe.

I woke feeling confused. Something had shaken me out of my sleep. A sound. I listened carefully, moving closer to the door. It wasn't them this time. Not human voices. Not the sounds of fighting I'd heard a few days ago, when they'd staggered back bloodied and charred. Not the muttering either. Theseus' persistent mumble, as she talked to something or someone only she could hear, had become a background noise, a low rumble which reverberated throughout The Collection. Useful, as it made her even easier to avoid. Worrying, because if she was losing her grip on sanity who knew what would follow. It wasn't that though. Nor was it the stifled sobbing of her girl, another recent development. She mostly cried at night when she thought Theseus couldn't hear. I felt sorry for her, and sometimes I would send Rohini to comfort her in my place. I couldn't risk showing myself to her. Her grasp on reality might have been slipping but I was more tangible than the voices in her head she told Theseus about. She'd probably have attacked first and asked questions later, if at all. They were alike in that way, something primitive and violent just below the surface.

The sound was low and harsh and came in short bursts. It was something almost felt rather than heard. it resonated, uncomfortably sexual. It reminded me of deer in rut. It spoke to me of pain and yearning. I crept out and followed the sound.

It was coming from the lowest floors. I knew they rarely went there. It had become something of a lair for Rohini. I don't think Theseus ever really bothered to go down there after her first cursory explorations when she arrived. It had become my habit to prop the cave door, the back door, open with a chair so Rohini could come and go. I'm certain I was the only one who ever opened or closed it. I might even have been the only other creature who knew it was there.

I could hear movement from the bathrooms so I knew it wasn't them. To be sure, though, I closed the door to the basement gardens behind me.

The grunts were closer together. Then they stopped. I paused, uncertainty suddenly taking over from the unthinking compulsion which had brought me down there. My fear faded as I heard the familiar heavy padding of Rohini's paws coming towards me.

Something wonderful. Impossible, I think, but wonderful.

This morning Rohini, the only tiger left in the world, proudly took me to see her newborn cub. I think she knows something we don't.

THE DREAMER

by Lisa Trott

Lisa is a product of a life lived across a few different countries, a couple of languages and a lot of geeky hobbies. She's an avid reader and writer of all things Fantasy, Sci-Fi and Folklore; the stranger the better. A late arrival to the worlds of tabletop roleplay and live action roleplay games, she used to enjoy running around muddy English fields pretending to be someone else but now is more likely to be found around a table playing Dungeons & Dragons. Currently living in the Pacific North West, she spends time with her husband and two adorably evil cats, playing video games and writing about weird and wonderful things.

My sincerest wish is that this warning does not find you too late. I cannot guess the will of The Collection, I only know that the knowledge I offer is of value to humanity. What's left of it. Because of this, I know it will reach you eventually.

To relate these matters in plain terms is the trickiest of undertakings. By the accumulation of truth, I have become trapped. The truth of now is not freeing. I know my end hunts me and I welcome it, for I have become far too wise without suffering the usual consequences. I have been an unwilling player, fashioned into a thorn in the side of unspeakable powers; I will now turn the amusement I have provided to better ends.

This is not just a warning, but also an introduction and a confession. I am the Dreamer and a thief.

The first thing to know is that I am supposed to be quite mad by now. I should be further down the paths of insanity than any mortal creature has likely had to tread and yet here I am, not dribbling or clawing out my eyes - for these are fates I have witnessed - and it is not as much as a blessing as it might sound.

I often wonder if the voices that accompany many of the moderately afflicted would be a comfort to me in the time that remains. Those that surround and support me seem placid enough to my eyes. Though I am certain they are not who they once were. They serve and gently mutter to themselves, sad spectres of this house. I like to imagine they do not suffer, these poor wretches I call 'The Hollow'. In some senses, they are the lucky ones.

I digress. Please forgive my ramblings and tangents. It has been a long time since I have written anything that felt my own.

You should know that our paths have crossed before, Curator, though I did all I could to prevent our coming into conflict. I have known several of you. I know how important you are. We each have our parts to play, though sometimes we can improvise a little. But the roles must always be filled.

And so to my confession, for without it the rest will seem a fabrication of the highest order. I have enclosed Dewy Decimal class references and other notes to help guide you, along with my ID cards, expired and useless as they now are, to prove authenticity. This is the first and last time I will ever write about this.

My rise in my chosen field was prodigious. I will spare you the tawdry details of my early years and advance to where things start to take shape. I was nominated to the USMA (perhaps you would know it as West Point) at the youngest admissible age by a well-respected Congresswoman who had somehow read about my 'astounding academic achievements' of preceding years; I was admitted with full scholarship.

I continued to impress my professors in both academic and physical endeavours, to a degree that prompted some of my peers to accusations cheating or bribing the teaching staff. I was the subject of several investigations and close examination. The faculty eventually concluded that I was gifted and it inspired jealousy amongst my more competitive contemporaries. Those who accused me without grounds were disciplined for behaviour unbecoming of a future officer in the United States Army.

I eventually became Senior Active-Duty Military Professor in Physics and Nuclear Engineering - 'PANE' as we would call it - a role that allowed me the best of both worlds. I went out on active-duty assignments and returned home to the comfort and structure of teaching alongside both military and civilian colleagues. My specialty, talent and dedication to the service garnered me more attention, eventually landing an advisory role serving the Joint Chiefs of Staff. I whispered into the ears of powerful people and they listened.

Such meteoric rises are perhaps a handful in each generation. My muse whispered to me in my sleep, instilling brilliant ideas and complex concepts that did not fade after waking. In dreams I made real progress, freed of the waking world's chains. A shadow danced beside me in my Dreamland - it had been there ever since I could remember - advising and improving me. I assumed it was part of me, my subconscious, more present and accessible than in most, which allowed me the great leaps and bounds I accomplished. In my early years. It called me Dreamer and told me that my potential was limitless.

As I drew even closer to power things changed, though I was not aware at the time. I advised with conviction, confident in my achievements and where they had taken me - one of the most senior officers in the country. Then, with one awful tip of a domino, I watched horrified as the delicate framework of the world swiftly collapsed.

Somehow, I slept the night before the Cold. As we stood on the brink of our cleverly wrought abyss, my shadow came to thank me and said that my work was not done yet.

I am the Dreamer, perhaps one of many, and I helped destroy everything.

The shadow of my Dreamland still urges me to act. It instructs me on when to use the antikythera to best effect. I am certain you are familiar with this device, though perhaps not the intricacies of how it works. Do not panic, friend, it is not yours to which I refer. Another was lost in time and my shadow guided me to it. The stars govern the shadowkind, and something of them powers the device.

Hold tight to that morsel, Curator. I believe the shadow to have been fleetingly careless in letting it slip. Remember the stars, for if they hold the power it implied, we may yet break free of this cursed future our powers so gleefully ran towards.

Imagine me as a subtle weapon. I inflict a thousand tiny cuts upon its kin. Such injuries are harmless to them, of course. It is merely a game amongst their kind. Perhaps I am better described as source of amusing frustration. I think they miss the days of the Cold War. Some never got to play puppet-master, so now new fields of battle must be found.

I seek them out. I steal their secrets, sometimes their possessions or people, so my shadow may better understand its kin and weaken them before it truly arrives here. It has somehow insulated my mind from the horrors I have witnessed. I suspect that, as I dream, it alters my perception so that I only remember useful things. But I feel madness scratching unseen in the corners. I am its scrying-glass, and I tire of it. My soul is in tatters. I have been this for too long.

I mentioned that our roles must always be filled. This is a pivotal part of plans and schemes greater than us both, Curator. Sometimes we are able to choose who takes on our mantle; sometimes others choose and humanity takes a step closer to extinction. I have not made an effort to select the next Dreamer, and for that I am sorry. I have no courage left to willingly inflict this existence on anyone. I can only hope that they are kinder and less foolish than I have been, quicker to turn their position to the benefit of humanity than I was.

Curator, be wary of them. Look for signs. I hope, in your current incarnation, that you have not had the misfortune of encountering one of my shadow's kin. Avoiding them becomes harder every day. They continue to journey here, now that they understand the nature of this place and know the way is clear.

Do not, under any circumstances, seek me out. If you ever lay your hands upon a doorway you do not recognise, run. Run as fast and as far as you can, run to The Collection and leave. Do not go inside - no one will welcome you. I will not be there and I cannot guarantee who will be. I cannot say if the next Dreamer will mean you harm. I have always tried to ignore what happens to trespassers. There are more of The Hollow here now than when I began.

Humans are all the same to its mind. We are cattle to be herded. If it understood how important you were to rebuilding humanity, perhaps it would make more of an effort to corral you. Let's not give it, or the others, any excuse to become aware of that, shall we?

The following references should help you learn more about my work before the Cold. The work that made the Cold.

Class 300, Social Sciences
- 350 Public administration & military science
  - 355 Military science > Ammunition > Warheads

Class 500, Science
- 530 Physics
  - 539 Modern physics > Nuclear physics
- 540 Chemistry
  - 541 Physical chemistry > Nuclear chemistry

In the envelope you will find the notes I mentioned. They are the last known locations of a great number of my shadow's kin. I am sorry I did not have time to overlay them on a map. I have included descriptions of their abilities and attributes where possible.

Do I fool myself into thinking that this is not too late? We have been doing this for centuries, our warnings and wisdom unheard or unheeded. Everything was twisted to their purpose long before I was born. How long have we been puppets? Could we have ever cut their cords and survived? No matter. We are past the point of no return.

Goodbye.

Gen. Avery J. Kelley
Chief of Staff of the United States Army

THE WATCHMAKER

by Ian Thomas

Ian is a writer, programmer, and games developer. He's worked in interactive television, education, puppet-making, film, publishing, live events, and the games industry, where he's helped bring to life games such as the existential horror SOMA, the live-action adventure The Bunker, and a wide variety of other titles from LittleBigPlanet to LEGO. He's written computer games, action movies, interactive fiction, and children's books about Cthulhu. He is co-director of Talespinners, a story-for-games company that helps developers create, polish, and deliver their narrative.

Night, but not dark. Makeshift lights hung threaded over corrugated rooftops, clouded jam jars dimming and brightening in spastic flickers, haloed by the drizzle. Something sputtered and rattled in time with the lights. A generator; this settlement had a generator.

"Hello?" Her voice reverberated off sheet metal walls. No reply.

She hugged the box tight to her, trying to keep it from the worst of the rain. The gate in front of her was a heavy slab of iron, perhaps cut from the bed of a truck. Which meant that here, they could cut iron. This must be the place.

Something shifted in the darkness to her right, its shadow flexing with the flickering of the lights. She'd taken two panicked steps back before she realised it was Rohini. The shape coughed an unhappy bass rumble, discontent with damp fur.

"I know," she said. "I won't be long. I think."

She stepped to the door, reached up, and rattled the chain that hung from an upturned tin bucket. The resulting clatter drove Rohini back into the night.

A hatch opened in the wall to the left of the door. She glimpsed matted hair and stained teeth. "'Tis it?" The voice was young, a boy.

"I'm here to see the Watchmaker."

"Who're yeh?"

"I... I'm the Curator."

Whispered consultation, and then, "Yer not."

"I'm the new Curator."

"Prove't."

She stood there, rain dripping down her face, blank, starting to shiver. Then: "Rohini?"

He came to lean against her leg, heavy, huffing. She put her hand down to stroke the coarse fur at the back of the tiger's neck.

Behind the hatch, drawn breath, more whispering, until, finally: "Aye."

A clang as the hatch shut. An ominous grating of iron. Then, incongruously, high-pitched mouse squeaks as the door eased open supported on a single wheel. She buried the smile.

Two small shapes, both with thornbush hair, were outlined against a dim light. She could just catch the glitter of eyes.

"Rohini, stay." The weight butted her leg, frustrated. "Please?" He huffed again, and padded, steaming, back into the dark.

"C'mon," said the taller of the two, a boy of perhaps twelve. He gestured with a gun, a revolver. There was nothing rusted about it - the metal gleamed in the light, etched with delicate traceries of thorns and flowers. Oh yes, this was the place. "We'll take yeh through."

It was a small shanty village, a mish-mash of hovels, wood and metal stacked on top of each other and life happening in the spaces between, like in so many refugee towns. But if you knew what to look for there was plenty of evidence. Jars of light strung across the street. A hand-pump, which meant someone knew how to craft that mechanism. A grindstone, foot-pedal operated. And there, high on a centrepiece built of old tyres and scaffolding, a great pale-faced clock, the copper pendulum below it carving up the rain into neat slices. She could hear the clack, the whirr, over the faint chug of the generator, the heartbeat of the sleeping settlement.

She'd glimpsed huddled forms, bundled up in blankets in the nooks and crannies of the shacks. But no one else was on the street save her two companions.

"What's he like?" she found herself asking.

The boy with the gun eyed her with suspicion. "Old."

"Oldest," chimed in the other, most likely a girl, a dark-skinned creature with startling blue eyes. "Older'n you. Older'n my dad, even."

"Where's the other Curator?" asked the boy. "She gave me a song."

"A song?"

He stared at her hard for a moment, then opened a leather bag and pulled out a piece of paper, folded and grimy. She took it carefully, judging that he considered it precious, and unfolded it.

The writing was in neat pencil in a hand she recognised. She scanned the lines and laughed. "You can read? You know the song?"

"Can't read. Know it, tho'. She sang it me, an' I remembered." He tapped his forehead.

"I know it," she said. "She had a few songs - this was one. She left it to me, along with a means to hear it." She folded the paper and handed it to him. As he took it she hummed the first bar, then started singing. The boy joined in, and by the time they reached the Watchmaker's house the girl was dancing along.

* * *

She'd pictured a room of delicate mechanisms, of clocks, cogs and springs, and indeed there were a fair few such things crammed into corners and dangling from shelves. But she hadn't counted on the twisted iron girders and blackened pistons; the cams and the flywheels; the cracked cases of old radios; streetlamps, ceramic insulators, pulleys, engines, barrels, bottles and even old toys. It was a junk room stacked haphazardly in teetering piles, metal highlights gleaming in the firelight. And this heat, the heat of the place! It all came from the furnace, where mechanical bellows heaved and puffed.

Nor was this how she'd pictured the Watchmaker. She'd seen him as a wizened old man with spectacles, grandfatherly, delicately picking apart a mechanism with a thin probe.

"Hello?"

He turned at her voice, this barrel-chested man, and grunted in surprise. He held up a gauntleted hand, gesturing her to wait, and turned back to his work.

He was stripped to the waist save for a heavy canvas apron, his skin thick with soot and sweat from the forge. He was near-bald, save for two tufts of stubble above his ears. He brought down the hammer - *once*-bounce-twice - on the glowing bar he held pinned in tongs. Again: *once*-bounce-twice. Spark. *Once*-bounce-twice. Then he thrust the bar into water and steam hissed, clouding them both.

She coughed at the taste of it.

"It'll be a pry-bar," he said. "Sometimes brute force is all that'll do. You're the Curator, now?"

"How did you-"

"The box," he said. He'd set aside the work, and was pulling off his gauntlets. His eyes were deep, dark, in a lined face whose age was impossible to guess, other than to say he was past his youth. A weathered oak, stern, unsmiling.

"The box! Yes." She'd forgotten she held it, and thrust it out to him hurriedly. He took it without a change in expression, set it down, and began to untie the cords around it.

"She told you what to do, then, in case of trouble? Told you the price?"

"I found a note."

He nodded, wiped his hands carefully with a rag, and then pulled the books from the box and spread them out on the workbench to study them.

It was a wide range of titles: *Haynes Owner's Manual for the Vauxhall Viva HC*, the *Cyclopedia of Applied Electricity Vol 6*, *Basic Naval Architecture, KC Barnaby - 1954*, and other tomes all drawn at random from section 620-629 following the previous Curator's instructions. And the last was a slim volume quite unlike the others. His hand hovered above it reverently; then he picked it up and turned it over and studied the writing on the back, brow slightly furrowed.

Had it been a joke, the book from 823? She'd thought so when she'd read Theseus's note. But when he set it down again with a satisfied grunt, she realised it was exactly what had been asked for.

He reached up to a high shelf above her head and pulled down other volumes. She recognised the titles; these were missing books from the engineering section.

He saw her expression. "Returns," he said. "You didn't think I kept them? The old man wouldn't have been happy with that." He stroked a tattered spine. "I'll miss these, though. Old friends. It's been a while since your predecessor was here."

One by one, he placed them in the box instead of the books she'd brought, then paused with the last book in his hand. She could see a title on the spine; it was also from 823, the previous book in the series. He stood with it a moment; then: "I'll take a minute, if you don't mind?"

"Of course," she said, confused.

He fumbled out spectacles from the pocket of his apron and set them on his nose, looking suddenly much older. He opened the book to the last few pages and traced the words with a finger. Then he smiled for the first time.

"Hah! Jane changed places with Carlotta! I thought it might be that!"

He ignored her confusion and carried on reading, skimming, turning pages. She bore the silence, knowing how much was at stake - this was a man she didn't want to upset.

A snap as he closed the book. "Thank you," he said. "I never know how long it'll be before one of your kind is here, so I don't finish them, you see. I stop before the mystery is spoiled, and I read and re-read again. Sometimes I'll read them to my daughter, and we'll talk about our theories. She is more often correct than I am, I'm ashamed to say."

He laid *Lord Edgeware Dies* in the box with the other returning books, and then tied it up with the cords and set it aside.

"Now. The problem?" he said.

"Oh! Yes, sorry." She reached into her pocket, pulled out a leather bag, and laid its contents on the workbench. A flat golden disk with irregular pins dotting its edges and a fine tracery of engraving across the front. He picked it up and studied it.

"Ah. I've seen this one before, have I not? Yes... it's thinned with use, see here, and that's set the balance off. It's wearing on these two pins. The spare's all right?"

"Well, it got me here. Will it take long to mend?"

"This won't mend. But I've a copy of it from the moulds I took; it was part of the bargain. I always keep another on hand. Besides," and the corner of his mouth crooked up, "I'm still trying to make my version of the damned thing work. Wait there."

He unbolted a heavy door and stepped through. She heard his hobnails clack on a wooden floor, and then there was silence, which stretched.

Something stirred by her head. She stepped back, heart hammering, and then realised it was a bird on a perch hanging from the roof. The little creature flapped its wings again with a whirr, then opened its beak and gave a wheezy chirrup that was slightly out of time with its movements. It was dull and rust-coloured, save for a patch of fresh copper on the feathers of its chest. It gave two more chirrups, flickered its wings, and then sat stone still.

The lights went out.

She heard the Watchmaker's muffled swearing, and then he was back in the room, outlined by the red glow of the forge. "Generator's out," he said, picking up a canister from under a table. "Wait. Touch nothing."

He went out the way she'd come in.

Touch nothing. Of course, her fingers itched.

Now her eyes had grown accustomed to the gloom, she realised there was another glow, not from the forge. A doorway at the back of the room, covered with a tattered curtain. She resisted her curiosity for a moment, congratulated herself, but then found that, somehow, her feet had taken her there anyway.

She twitched aside the curtain. The glow came from a fire in a hearth. In front of it, a girl was lying on a rug, a book spread out in front of her, her chin pillowed on her hands, her heels kicking lazily. She reached out and turned a page. In the firelight, the Curator saw words, and a picture of a lion. It wasn't a book she knew.

"What are you reading?"

At the sound, the girl froze, then turned slowly to look at her. Her expression was calm, uncurious, but her dark eyes were watchful. She didn't reply.

The Curator tried again. "The book? I was wondering what it was?"

The girl held her gaze for perhaps a second, saying nothing. Then she turned back to her reading. Her heels started kicking again.

The Curator gave it up as a bad job, and went back to wait in the dark.

* * *

"Done," said the Watchmaker, rasping off a final speck of brass with a file. The generator chugged away again without complaint; if anything, the light seemed brighter. He handed her the replacement disk, gleaming and polished, with no sign of the wear of the other.

"Thank you," she said. "I'd best be on my way. My companion can be impatient."

He nodded. "I'll see you again, I'm sure. You will be welcome. Return -

but not too soon, for I've much to digest." He glanced at the slim volume and smiled again. "And my daughter and I have new mysteries to solve."

She made the disk safe, then picked up the box, and he saw her out into the night.

"It's a bloody big cat," said the boy. "What's it eat?"

"It's a tiger. It eats… far too much, as it happens."

"Hope you've brought summat for it. It's bin carryin' on out there. Growlin' and such. Thought I'd have to pop 'im. Bang!" He waved the gun.

"I think that might just make him angry."

"Well, we're here," said the boy, stepping to one side of the gate and pulling a lever. It squeaked open.

"Thank you," she said. "Maybe next time I'll bring you a new song."

He shrugged. "I've got one. Don't see as how I need another."

"Thank the Watchmaker and his daughter for their hospitality, won't you?"

A quizzical look. "Daughter? He ain't got a daughter. Did once, maybe, years back, but nah, not no more."

She stood there a moment, the flesh of her scalp crawling, and then, finally, swallowed. "Well. Thank him, anyway."

As she walked away through the drizzle, Rohini by her side, the box under her arm and the replacement piece for the Antikythera device safe in a pocket, she couldn't help hear the song that Theseus had given to the boy. The last Curator must have known, must have chosen it deliberately. It was one of the disks left out in its paper cover in the alcove of the Music section. She'd listened to it; the music was nice enough, but the lyrics had always disturbed her.

She could picture the record itself - silver writing on a green background. Lettering: 'Columbia', '45-DB 4306', "(from film Serious Charge)", "Cliff Richard and the Drifters". And then that title.

THE CURATOR

by Stephen McGreal

Stephen McGreal is a prolific writer, but not generally a writer of fiction. In his day job, he writes code for video games. In his alter-ego as a bard in a Live Role Play system, he writes smutty and satirical (and occasionally serious) songs. As a father of two young boys, he helps them to write things like "The cat sat on the mat". This is the first time he has written fiction that has been published - which means that this is also the first time he has written a bio.

Hank leapt with a start from the battered armchair, eyes adjusting to the dusk, as Winston continued barking and pawing at the window. The old German Shepherd seemed agitated by something out in the patch of woods to the east of the ramshackle farmhouse.

Over the years Winston had proved his use time and again, sounding the alarm when bandits came wandering onto the farmstead looking to take whatever they could. A row of shallow graves at the bottom of the orchard stood as testament to Hank's opinion of them. He'd often thought it stupid to keep calling it the orchard, given no trees grew in there; just a handful of dead trunks slowly being devoured by fungus. But a name's a name. It was the orchard and he'd be damned if he'd start calling it the graveyard, even if that's what it had become.

The bandit attacks had gotten less frequent though, and Hank hadn't had an unexpected visitor in two or three years, now. If bandits were out looking for rich pickings, rural Wisconsin wasn't likely to be their first choice of destination. Maybe Winston had taken to barking at shadows instead. Maybe there were bears out in the woods. Not that Hank'd be able to see anything amongst the trees at this time of the evening. He went to look anyway.

"Mary!" He fumbled for the shotgun propped up by the door, not taking his eyes away from the window. "Mary, you need to come see this!"

"What? Hank, why have you and Winston gotta be making such a racket down here?" Mary came into the living room, a sputtering candlestick in one hand and clutching a shawl around her thin shoulders with the other. "You know Sophie needs her rest, and... Oh."

The last of the day's sunlight was fading, turning the woods into a smear of black below a bloated, watery-looking moon. And impossibly, at the edge of the tree-line, was a *doorway*. A rectangle of tiny stars.

There was a figure. Someone strolling from the doorway and picking their way across the field. The house vibrated with Winston's barks as the figure swung open the garden gate. Hank clutched the shotgun and pressed himself against the wall beside the door.

Rat-a-tat-tat.

Silence. Winston stared at the door, ears down. Hank could hear his own breathing, blood pounding in his ears. A ragged, hacking cough from upstairs.

Rat-a-tat-tat.

"Who the hell is it?" bellowed Hank. "What do you want? We got nothing here for you, so you best get the fuck off my property, or I'll-"

"Relax, friend," came the voice from the other side of the door. A man, calm and well-spoken. "I'm not here to rob you. I'm here to help you. Please, open the door."

Hank reached for the doorknob, twisted it, then slammed the door wide open, bringing the shotgun to bear on the stranger's face. The man smiled. He was tall and slender, his height accentuated by a battered top hat. His face was deeply lined, a maze of creases surrounding his twinkling eyes. It was hard to guess at his age – he might have been forty, or twice that. He wore a tweed jacket and had leather satchel slung over one shoulder. Perched on the other shoulder was a large crow, which regarded the barrel of the shotgun with a cool detached curiosity. Winston padded silently forward and the man bent down to scratch him behind the ears.

"You won't be needing the gun. I'm unarmed, and I mean you no harm. May I come in?"

Hank, hands shaking, lowered the barrel and stood aside. He wasn't sure why. He wasn't used to visitors, at least not the friendly kind, but the man seemed harmless enough and Winston was a pretty good judge of character. Mary stood by the fireplace, anxious and curious.

"Allow me to introduce myself," said the stranger, stepping into the farmhouse and looking around as if he was appraising the humble room's aesthetics. "I am The Curator."

"The... The what now?"

"The Curator – at your service. And my associate here is Titus." He indicated the crow, which cawed. "Tell me, have you ever heard of The Collection?"

"You mean that magic flying library thing? It's a fairy story. Somethin' you tell to the little'uns when you tuck 'em into bed."

The Curator smiled. "It's a wonderful story, isn't it? Something to tell the little'uns, as you say, to give them some hope. Knowing there is a library somewhere, a store of all the knowledge and wisdom from before the Cold. Knowing that it is being used, piece by piece, one act of kindness at a time, to *rebuild* this world, our civilisation. Our very humanity!" The Curator leaned towards Hank, and in a conspiratorial tone continued "It doesn't fly, of course. That would be a nonsense. But it does *move*. The entrance moves from place to place, to where it is needed most."

"Now, what in the hell is all this about, mister?' growled Hank, tightening the grip on the shotgun. "Why are you in my house, talking about this Collection horseshit? Everyone knows it's a myth."

The Curator seemed amused. "Is it? So how do you explain *that*?" He pointed through the window to the twinkling rectangle of light in the woods. "Has anyone ever arrived at your house in this manner before?"

"Well... no," conceded Hank. "But-"

"Think about it – what should I call you?"

"Hank."

"Think about it, Hank. Did you ever read about The Collection in some book of children's tales? Or did you hear it through whispers, rumours, from the wind itself? It's a story told by adults, and they tell it because it's true. Did you really think that before the Cold, when the world was going crazy, there wasn't anyone planning for humanity's future? Of course they were! Knowledge fades fast without the written word to disseminate it. There are those of us out there determined that Humanity is not going to just lie down and accept a long slow death in the Cold. Can you read, Hank?"

"Sure. Not much call for it these days, mind."

"Excellent. Yes, precisely my point. When is the last time you saw a book?"

"Damned if I know. Ten years? Fifteen? Everyone burned whatever they could find in those first few years just to stay alive."

The Curator slung his satchel off his shoulder and placed it with theatrical care on a table. He began carefully pulling out books and placing them on the table. They looked old – definitely from before the Cold – dog-eared and yellowed, with fading covers, loose pages and cracked spines. But they were books. Half a dozen of them.

"Come," said The Curator. "Come and see."

He picked up the books tenderly, like ancient relics, and opened them at random pages to show Hank their contents. There was some kind of manual for the maintenance of a vehicle called a Land Rover, filled with cutaway diagrams of engines; an illustrated book about spotting different kinds of berries and fungus; some kind of physics textbook with equations and diagrams of weights hanging from pulleys; a very old-looking book hand-written in a language Hank didn't understand, the spidery text wrapped around drawings of five-pointed stars and other strange symbols; something that looked like a novel, about the actions of a Scottish nobleman; and

"This," said The Curator, "may be of interest. 'Farming Techniques Through The Ages'. You see, The Collection always sends me where I'm needed. And, Hank, if I had to guess, I'd say you've been struggling a bit with this farm you've got here. I don't mean any offence, I'm sure you're a very skilled farmer, but-"

"It's true," sighed Hank. "That darned ash rains down and it just sucks all the goodness out of the soil. Whole fields where nothing grows. We're still getting some crops, but they're small, sickly. Choked up by weeds. I don't know how we're going to get through next winter."

"Exactly!" said The Curator, enthusiastically. "I can help you with that. The answer probably isn't in this exact book, of course. These are just some samples that I brought to show you. But The Collection has a whole section on farming techniques. And a laboratory, too. If I can take some of the grains you've been growing, and a soil sample, I can test those, cross-reference them with geographic and climate information, and find the specific reference materials to help you repair these fields and get the crops growing again. I'll make a copy of the information for you."

"Really? You can do that?"

The sound of a major coughing fit erupted from upstairs. Mary rushed from the room and thundered up the stairs.

"What was that?" inquired The Curator.

"Sophie. Our daughter. She's real sick. We don't know what to do."

"Aha!" exclaimed the stranger. "You see? The Collection really has sent me to you in your hour of need! May I see her?"

The Curator made his way into the small, dimly-lit bedroom. Mary sat beside the bed, one hand holding her teenage daughter's and the other gently sweeping sweat-slicked strands of hair from her face. Sophie's skin was pale and pock-marked with angry-looking blisters. She was motionless save for the movement of her chest taking in rapid, shallow breaths. A bucket stood on the floor beside the bed, its bottom filled with a foul-smelling liquid. As the Curator approached he lifted his hand to where Titus was perched. The crow hopped onto his fingers and he transferred it to the bed. Titus walked gingerly across the bedsheets and examined the girl's face. Sophie's eyes were half open but she didn't acknowledge her visitors.

"How long has she been like this?"

"Couple of weeks. First the cough. Then she started complaining about feeling tired all the time. Then it started getting worse. Now, what'n the hell is your damned *bird* doing to her?"

"Titus is examining her to ascertain the nature of her ailment, and how we might be able to help. Crows are very intelligent creatures with very sharp senses, and this one has had a lifetime of training as my assistant. He may not look like much to you, but he serves as a librarian, a physician, and my companion. Some have even been moved to speculate if he might be described as my familiar."

"Well," said Hank eyeing the bird with some scepticism, as if afraid that at any moment it might peck out Sophie's eyes, "I heard that the curator of The Collection had some kind of cat, not a bird. For that matter, I heard the curator was a woman."

The stranger smiled. "Ah, Hank. The Collection has had several curators over the years, each with a predilection for animal companions. I am merely the current one. I daresay one of my predecessors was indeed a woman with a cat. It's a dangerous business, you see – a dangerous world out there, and many people would try to use The Collection for their own ends. We curators are sworn to defend humanity's last great store of knowledge with our lives, and several have paid that price. I hope to avoid following in their footsteps, of course. And The Collection has its own means of self-defense."

As Hank attempted to process this information, Titus cawed again and look expectantly at the Curator.

"Yes, Titus," he said. "Yes, of course. I believe we have some in my satchel – oh, I seem to have left it downstairs. Would you be a good fellow and fetch it for me?" In a flurry of feathers that made Mary leap out of her seat, the crow launched itself from the bed and through the door. "I have some medication in my bag," explained the Curator. "It won't cure her, but it should ease the fever and coughing for a short time. You're extremely lucky we arrived when we did – as I'm sure you're acutely aware, Sophie's situation is very serious. The good news is that Titus believes it is not too late to save her. There is a small pharmacy within The Collection, medicines that other people have donated in exchange for information. I believe we have the cure she needs in stock. You can consider the medicine that Titus is bringing from my bag as a gift, to give your family some peace of mind whilst we discuss the delicate matter of payment."

"Payment?" spluttered Hank, his face reddening. "So you *do* want somethin' from us! Well we ain't got shit. Look around you, can't you see that?"

The Curator spread his hands wide in a gesture of conciliation. "Please. Hank. The Collection demands that I operate under certain rules. I can't simply *give* things away, much as I'd like to. We have running costs. We have to trade for useful items like the pharmaceuticals. We have to maintain the books. We have to power the door to keep moving, the lights so we can even find the right books in there, let alone read them. I'm going to make copies of the pertinent farming materials for you – do you have any idea how expensive paper is? And Titus and I have to eat, of course. But look at what you're getting! Without the farming materials your family will starve. You said it yourself. *With* those materials, you will not only survive, but you can grow enough food to sell at your local market, feed your neighbours and earn some favours. Likewise, without medication..." The Curator's voice tailed off and his eyes moved towards the bed, full of sadness and pity.

"But what can we pay you with?" Hank demanded, his voice tinged with panic. "Like I said, we got nothin'!"

Titus hopped back through the doorway, a small bottle of pills in his beak. The Curator picked the bird up, deposited it on its shoulder, and took the bottle. "Oh, don't worry," he said, examining the label on the bottle. "'From each according to his ability, to each according to their needs.' The payment need not be extortionate, merely adequate. For instance, I noticed you have a pickup truck in the yard. Is there any gas in that? Any spare shells for that shotgun of yours?" He shook the bottle and the pills rattled loudly inside. "What do you say, Hank?"

***

The man who called himself the Curator whistled as he walked towards his star-lined doorway in the woods. The gasoline he had siphoned from the truck sloshed pleasingly in the jerry-can, and the box of shotgun shells nestled in his satchel beside a jewellery box that Titus had quietly purloined on the way to fetch the sugar pills. The fuel would keep his small portable generator running, the one that powered the fairy lights strung around the collapsible wooden door frame he had built. The jewellery looked like it would fetch a pretty price at the right market - enough to feed him, his crow, and the horse that transported them across the forgotten parts of America for quite some time. It might even buy him a couple of new books to show people, if he could find any. He wondered whether he'd be able to track down an impressive-looking medical reference book of some sort. The shells? He'd find a use for them. Now all he had to do was collapse the door quickly, get it onto the cart that was hidden in the woods, then get away from this excuse for a farm before the dumb hicks cottoned on that he wasn't coming back.

As he approached the frame, the door swung open and filled the clearing with light. The Curator froze in horror and confusion.

I never put a door into that frame, he thought, *not worth the effort.*

But now, there was a door. And the silhouette of a woman stepping out of it, holding a rifle. Through the doorway he could see walls, lights, as if the doorway opened into a room.

Impossible!

There was another figure silhouetted behind the woman. Lithe, predatory. A cat – no, a fucking *tiger.* A heavy stillness hung in the air as the woman looked at him, assessed him. Then she turned around, examined the door frame, the fairy lights.

"Let me guess," said the woman, a hint of amusement in her voice. "You're the Great and Mighty Curator, right? I've wanted to meet you ever since I heard about you, but the antikythera doesn't just take me wherever I want to go. You actually built a *doorway?* And you carry it around with you?

Do you have the slightest idea how dangerous that is? At the very least, you should have been expecting a visit from me someday."

Titus' claws dug deeply, painfully into the man's shoulder as the enormous tiger eyed it hungrily, tongue curling against its brutal-looking teeth.

"So," said the woman. "I think it's time that you and I had a little chat."

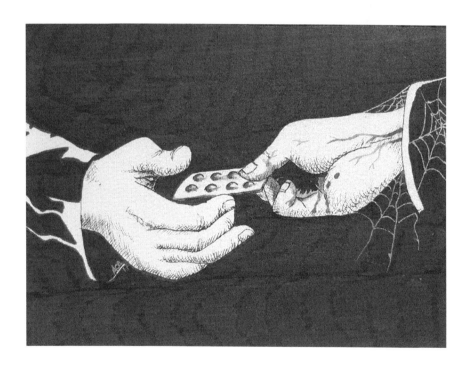

QUEEN OF DANCERS

by Adrian Waite

Adrian hails from the land of Yorkshire and enjoys nothing more than a roast dinner covered in divine gravy whilst writing about adventurers slaying monsters.

He rummaged through the debris. Anything would do as long as it was dry enough to burn. It was so cold, all the time. His gloves were old, battered thin and holey. He tugged them off carefully and gave them to Toby anyway. The boy balled little white fists up in the wool and kept shivering.

"I'll have a fire going soon," he promised. "Just a few more minutes. You stay there like a good boy for me and read your book."

"Yes, Dad."

The voice was a trembling thread, exhausted obedience. He kicked a spot clear of snow and fumbled with the meagre kindling. The firesteel sparked five, six, seven times before he could get it to catch, blowing carefully and sheltering it with numb hands.

"There we are," he said at last, sitting back on his heels. "Isn't that better?"

"Yes, Dad." Toby sounded sleepy, voice no longer shaking. "I think the Cold is going away now."

He turned. The boy was slumped to one side, eyelids drooping. The brightly coloured picture book lay spine-up in the snow, wet soaking into its precious paper pages. The gloves were balled up next to it.

He took Toby's limp fingers gently, as if they were icicles that might snap. "Why did you take your gloves off, son?"

"M'hands don' hurt anymore."

He unzipped his coat and drew his son close, between his own body heat and the meagre fire. He rubbed one palm over Toby's thin chest, trying to stimulate warmth. It was too cold for tears. They were all frozen, grey and scarred over in the ducts.

"Shall we read your story?" he said roughly, reaching for the sodden book. "Would you like that?" He held it in front of Toby. A bright city spread across its pages, spires rising up in primary colours into an ashless sky, utterly alien to the grey wreckage of civilisation that surrounded them. "Can you tell me how it starts, Toby? Come on, read with me. Once…?"

"Once 'ponna time," the boy mumbled, words slurring.

"Good boy. Keep going for me. Come on."

"Was a queen."

"That's right." He turned the page, to where a woman spun in a whirl of long black hair and long red skirts. "The queen loved to dance. Just like your mum did."

A thin white hand reached out to touch the picture then dropped, suddenly heavy. "Looks like Mum?"

"Yes." He swallowed once, and dragged in air. "Do you remember Mum's hair? She used to tickle you with the ends." It had all fallen out before she died. He hadn't let their son see her after that. The sickness corrupting her skin, her lungs, her muscles. He'd promised to keep Toby alive. It was the last thing he'd said that she heard.

"'M sleepy," Toby whispered.

"You can't sleep yet." The kindling collapsed into itself and the fire guttered. He carefully set his son down and took off his coat, wrapping it around bony shoulders. "I need to fix the fire. Keep telling me the story. What did the queen do?"

The tumble of rocks and concrete was full of wind-sheltered alcoves where people had surely stopped for the night before. He kicked piles of rubble aside, hunting for anything that would burn.

"Keep reading, Toby," he called. "Nice and loud, so I can hear."

"She had a prince that she showed all her dancing to."

"Good boy. What was the prince called?" He moved on to the next group of rocks. There were the remains of an older fire here, lumps of charred wood not fully burned through. Enough for an hour at least. Would that be enough to get Toby's temperature up? It had to be. "I can't hear you, son. What was the prince called?"

"Toby."

"A good name for a prince." He rounded the rocks and crouched next to the dying fire, carefully coaxing it to feed on the blackened wood. "What happens next?"

"Danced."

He looked up at the breath of sound. Toby's eyes were closed, his face white as the snow that laid siege to them. He hurriedly pushed the last of the scavenged wood into the flames and dragged the bundle of coat and boy into his arms.

"That's right," he said gently, and pressed a kiss to the tangle of black curls. "They danced every day together."

"Tired, Dad."

"I know, son. Maybe we'll have better luck finding food tomorrow. Sleep now. Ssssh. It's okay." He rocked back and forth slowly, as Toby's breathing shallowed and softened. "It's okay. I've got you. It's all going to be alright."

The last thing to burn was the book. It didn't matter by then.

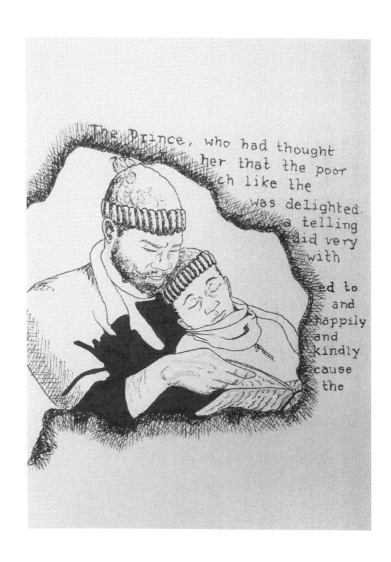

SANDALWOOD

by James Trott

James Trott is a British engineering leader for a big tech company. He's also a software developer, hacker, and all-round geek. His over-active childhood imagination fuelled nightmares and created a fascination with monsters which has never left him. That fascination forged a love of the hammer horror monsters, Disney villains, 80s horror movies, the works of Lovecraft and Geiger, and Dungeons and Dragons to name a few. All of which now inspire him to create games, and stories centred around monsters of his own, whether the friendly ones that live under the bed, or the old ones that lurk in the shadows.

The handle turned freely. Fresh oil soothed the squeaking of the gears and the antikythera sprung to life immediately at her hand's request, a heartfelt thank-you from the old man for the maintenance.

She'd often wondered why she personified it, or was it anthropomorphized? She always got those two confused, she'd have to make another trip to Class 4 to find out. She hated things being in disorder, especially her own thoughts.

"Old man", she whispered quietly to herself. "You've lived and seen more than a lifetime's worth haven't you, old friend."

If she was being honest, it was the most straightforward relationship she'd ever had with a man. Certainly, the only one she could rely on. All it asked for in return was the occasional drop of oil. Likely, it would be the last relationship too. The collection was what mattered now, and her care and curation of it came above all else.

"The collection must survive" she said aloud. She did that sometimes. Spoke out when she was alone, just to remind herself that she could and, sometimes, to hear a friendly voice in echoes.

She grabbed her small day-pack from beside her favourite armchair and threw it onto her back in a well-practiced motion. She reached down onto the plate that sat on the small table, next to the book she'd been reading the evening before. *The Odyssey* was one of her favourites. The story of the Greek king Odysseus and his long journey home after a war. She'd read it dozens, if not hundreds of times. It brought her comfort in the world, somehow made her feel less lonely. Less... hopeless. She wondered silently how many years it would be before she would see home again. If she did at all.

She scooped up the leftover meat she'd recently traded fresh vegetables for into her gloved hand, and tossed it up onto a high shelf two rows over. She'd only been able to eat half. Fatigue always made it hard for her to eat protein. She knew that maintaining nutrition was key but time was running short, and it wouldn't go to waste.

As she opened the door a gust of sharp, cold air roused her senses to alertness. She turned her head back just a half turn, to hear the loud syncopated rumbling emanating from the shelf above. She smiled to herself, closed the door and stepped out into the cold, dark alleyway.

She made her way through the narrow passages, marking walls and corners with a piece of chalk stone. Her other hand rested on the knife hilt concealed in her sleeve. Learning to mark had taken a while but losing the door once had been enough. Sleeping rough wasn't her favourite when it was necessity, but through her own stupidity? The cold and hunger that night had only served to exacerbate her fear that she had lost the collection forever or, worse, allowed it to fall into nefarious hands.

After several more twists and turns she found herself looking out onto a wide main thoroughfare, on a cool, clear, breezy day. Folks were clinging to wraps, shawls, scarfs and head coverings as they went about their day. The unmistakable scent of wood smoke permeated the air, spiralling into the sky above poorly maintained structures. She took in a lungful of the crisp cool air and stepped out onto the cobbles, moving like a fish through the noise and clutter of street traders, wagons, carts, and crowds.

She walked past a cart selling what passed as 'fruit', slightly browned, soft looking, some of which appeared to be mouldy. It was likely fine if you wiped it off before eating - it was old but bore none of the warning signs of being toxic. Apart from the mould, of course, but it was the blueish green kind so the worst you could expect was an upset stomach. She'd even read that the green kind could be turned into medicine with the right equipment,.

As she continued, her feet feeling the texture of the street underneath, breathing in the sights and smells of a new place, she came across a man stood upon a wooden crate. He gesticulated wildly as he proselytized to the passing crowds, who seemed to be ignoring him.

"The stigma of being a beggar," she thought, looking at the box in front of him, which contained a myriad of objects. "Or at least that is the intended illusion."

The things had likely been tossed in from passers-by: a few lumps of coal, the stale end of a loaf, and what appeared to be a silver whistle that glistened in the midday sun. He smelled foul, even from a good eight or ten feet away. Naked but for a poncho that was covered in indecipherable scrawlings of what she assumed was coal, and other things, slightly lighter but decidedly more unpleasant, in shades of red and brown.

"Think on all ye sheep, as you herd yourselves through the gates of their will, along the thoroughfare of their design. For even the wolf that walks among us is hunted by what it cannot hope to escape. The dark is come, and whether the forest of your hearth be verdant or desolate, there remains no shepherd to guard us from the horrors harvested from the seeds sown of the soul."

She found herself lost in the swirling pool of his words, the rhythm and delivery almost poetic. She awoke with a start as she collided with an oncoming pedestrian, falling backwards and landing with a sharp pain as a cobbled stone connected with her tail bone. She let out a squeal of pain and lifted her eyes. A man's face came into view.

"I'm so terribly sorry" he exclaimed, removing a leather glove and extending a remarkably clean, manicured hand toward her.

He was wearing a long black, smart coat that hung just above ankle height. He wore black, shiny shoes, also oddly clean, and a purple suit the same shade as the plums ripening in The Collection's basement.

She accepted the hand and he effortlessly pulled her to her feet, his clothing apparently hiding an abundance of strength . Her head swam and her vision went blurry. She felt like she might faint as memories rushed through her mind: the street, the beggar, the alleyways, the marks on the wall, the door, the meat, the book, the plate, the old man, the gears, the oil, the odyssey...

Her vision snapped into sharp focus as the headiness evaporated. She was on her feet, still holding the hand of the stranger who was uncomfortably close. He smelled wonderful, like spices toasting in brazier. Like sandalwood.

Sandalwood was ingrained somewhere deep inside her. It reminded her of her father. She'd forgotten what he looked like but that smell... He would mix his own oil for his beard, stirring the dust of sandalwood into it. She took in a deep breath, hoping to hold it in like a hound with a scent, then stepped back.

"No, no, please, it was my fault. I wasn't looking where I was going."

Deep dark grey eyes peered back at her from an immaculately groomed face. "I insist, the fault is entirely mine, miss...?"

She opened her mouth, but was interrupted as the beggar jumped between them and began yelling into her face.

"His fetid touch condemns us all! Low rich crystal water is poured upon seeds sown across deep furrows of fertile soil. We must flee before the darkness settles upon us. DOOM! DOOM has come and the nightmare begins its slow descent as madness grows." He turned to the stranger in the purple suit. "How dare you, sir, to harm a lady, so brazen in the day. Be gone, abominable one!"

The stranger struck the beggar with the back of his still gloved hand, knocking him to the floor. The beggar slid across the cobbles with surprising force and collided with his box of meagre donations. Scrambling to his feet, he gathered his things and scampered away, disappearing into the bustling crowds.

The stranger's piercing gaze returned to her. "So sorry about that. Now where were we? Ah yes, your name?"

"Sorry, I don't give my name to strangers, not least violent ones. Especially ones who clearly have enough means not to need to employ such behaviour. ESPECIALLY over those who are in no position to do the same by way of return."

With that she gathered her pack and barged past him, allowing her shoulder to collide with him on the way. It hurt more than she had anticipated. He barely moved and she schooled her expression to hide the pain, not wanting him to have the satisfaction.

The stranger replaced his glove and called over his shoulder. "Farewell, then, milady."

She turned to face him. It was about time he heard some home truths about his sort and the world they lived in now. Her face was red with frustration and anger at the injustice, disparity and privilege she had just witnessed. But he was gone. She scanned the crowd but could spot no trace of him. Her shoulders slumped and she carried on her way.

A few dozen yards later, a hand reached out and lightly grasped her arm. A familiar stench emanated from the alleyway just to her right-hand side. "Apologies, and great thanks, for defending poor Ulus."

She turned to see the beggar cowering just inside the alley's opening. "It's ok," she said softly. "The haves like him should know better, though mayhap you yourself should pick your battles more carefully."

"Mayhap" he replied, opening and extending his other hand to reveal the shiny silver whistle. He spoke with a coherence and clarity she had not credited him with. "A gift, to express my gratitude. You'll need it more than old Ulus, and besides, I thought your ilk didn't simply gift assistance?"

She tried to push his offering away. "There are always exceptions, Ulus. And what do you mean by my ilk?"

The old beggar insisted, pressing the whistle into her hand and closing her fingers around it. She smiled and bowed her head slightly in thanks. "You, my dear, may call me Vincent, should our paths ever cross again. I know who you are or, rather, what you are. Easy enough when you know what you're looking at. I was fortunate enough to make the brief acquaintance of one of your predecessors … " His voice trailed off as he raised his eyes skyward, lost in thought. "… in another time, a different place… It seems a lifetime ago," he whispered as he began backing into the alleyway. His voice descended into an incoherent mutter. He gave a gentle smile that made the signs of age and time more apparent than before; years of experience, hardship and memory etched like an atlas across his face.

"Thank you again, Vincent" she said, as she reached into her pack, before throwing him the healthy apple she'd picked that morning. "In trade.

You probably remember that we can neither take nor give. So trade it is. Stay warm tonight."

He caught the apple and tipped his fingers toward her in a slight salute of thanks, before turning and walking around a corner. She slipped the chain of the long silver tube around her neck and tucked it into her shirt, before resuming her exploration of the city.

After another few hours or so exploring the main streets and thoroughfares she turned down a side-street and headed into the warren of alleyways that interconnected them. The main drag never had much - that's where everyone went, so that's where the normal, mundane everyday things were. The real gems, the secret shops, and hidden treasures, were always off the beaten path. Besides, her methodical nature meant that not getting the lay of the land would not only leave her exposed if she needed to retreat in a hurry, but also leave her wondering if she had missed something. After a while exploring the maze of side-streets, she noticed a faint yet familiar smell, warm and savoury, a hint of sweetness mixed with smoke.

She followed it to a squat stone building with a domed roof, illuminated by flickering flames within. A small awning outside covered a table upon which sat loaves of fresh baked bread. She could see smoke billowing from a hole in the top of the dome, a mix of white and grey, swirling in eddies up and out over the rooftops. A tall, muscular man stood behind the table, arms folded across a dusty white apron, surveying the occasional passer-by.

"Is this a bakery?"

He raised a single eyebrow at her and barked "Does it look like a bakery?"

"Yes!" she said brightly, grinning from ear to ear. "And it smells like one too! I'd like to trade for one of your loaves please."

She loved bread, the smell, the texture, the taste. But it was so rare to come across good fresh bread. She'd wanted to make her own and had spent countless nights in Class 6, researching about baking. But flour was harder to come by than she'd imagined. No matter where she went, she could never find people who had it, or were willing to trade what small amount they had. She'd tried to get around the problem by making her own. There were plenty of books in Class 3 about agriculture before the cold. She -even managed to trade for some grain from a brewer. They always had grain = people might be starving but they would always trade for a drink to forget for a while. So long as there were taverns and speakeasies, brewers would have grain.

Conveniently, they also always had yeast of some variety. Though she'd learned that with just flour and water one could simply 'capture' yeast from the air. The grain she bartered for wasn't nearly enough to grind into a batch of flour so, after more study in Class 3, she'd tried to grow some more in the basement garden. She hadn't counted on how low the yield would be, and she estimated she could probably manage a half-dozen loaves if she re-planted the entire garden with grain. That was never going to work. So she'd ground down what she had, and had been feeding a small mason jar of flour and water every day to capture her yeast.

"What do you have to trade?" the man said loudly, as if he'd just had to repeat himself.

Her mind snapped back to attention, forcing out thoughts of delicious bread and failed experiments. She reached into her knapsack and retrieved a small wicker basket, wrapped in cloth. She leaned over the table and beckoned the man closer, lifting just the corner of the cloth.

"Are those strawberries?!" he exclaimed.

"Shhhhhh….." she hissed. "Do you want everyone to hear you?"

"Sorry. How many are in there?"

"A dozen."

"I don't have enough bread to make a fair trade."

She smiled wryly. She knew the value of what she was holding. She treasured them, savouring each sweet morsel every time she allowed herself to sparingly partake. That was the great thing about growing things underground. With the right conditions it was possible to grow anything, all year round.

"I'll take two loaves for them."

He tilted his head to one side, looking confused and slightly untrusting.

"I suspect you have something else I want."

"I am but a baker. I have a son to feed. Everything I have allows me to scrape my meagre living. What could I possibly have to trade that you would want?"

"I've heard a myth …" she said, lying. She'd done no such thing, she'd read about it. "… of a way to make bread from potatoes."

The man looked at her sternly, his nose just a few inches from hers, the basket between them. His face contorted into a knowing smile. "That's no myth."

He grasped the basket with both hands. Her grip tightened as she observed him, considering his intentions, and then released. He chuckled, then laughed, a deep, rolling belly laugh. Any sign of sternness he had previously possessed evaporated as his face turned pink and a wide smile spread across his visage. As he tucked the basket into a lockbox behind his table, he began to talk.

"My grandmother used to tell me stories of such baking. She made it for me once. Delicious! Different flavour, but bread nonetheless, and the most beautiful crispy crust you've ever tasted."

Her mouth watered at the mere thought of it. "So, you can tell me how to make it?"

"Of course. The recipes my grandmother passed down helped my mother found this bakery. When I came over age, she passed them to me. For such a bounty as you have offered, I'd be happy to give you a copy of the recipe in exchange."

Just then, rapid footsteps came running down the alleyway to one side.

"Dad! Dad!" A tall broad-shouldered boy, no older than 14 or 15, came into view, holding something large wrapped in a dirty blanket in his arms.

"My son," the baker said. "Emmet? Is everything ok?"

The lad's face was red, and he was wheezing and coughing as he came to a stop. "Dad, you have to help... I found her... I think she's dying."

The baker pulled back the cloth to reveal a small girl, around 7 years old, her face bright red and covered with beads of sweat. Steam rose from her body in the cold air.

"Bring her inside" he said, opening the door. "Put her on the table then take care of the stall."

The boy did as he was told, effortlessly placing the bundled-up girl onto a long kitchen table in a side room from the main bakery. The curator followed instinctively.

"I was heading back from the canal after my last sale on the barge moorings, and there she was, wrapped up in that blanket, whimpering like a dog, I didn't know what to do, Dad, so I brought her home."

The baker's lips pursed into a reassuring smile. "You did the right thing, lad. Go take care of the stall. We'll see what we can do for her."

The baker carefully peeled back the blanket. The girl was wearing a simple white linen dress with a blue ribbon around the waist. She was sopping wet, but the curator couldn't tell if it was from sweat, or something else. The baker felt her brow.

"She's as hot as my oven." He looked hopefully at the curator. "Can you help her?"

She felt the young girl's head. This was a fever, she'd seen them before and learned about them in the books of Class 6. The girl's breath was faint and fading.

"I can. In fact I think I have something for it, but you'll have to trade me. The Collection, you see... I can't just go giving things out."

His eyes widened at a sudden realization. He looked down at the little girl. "Would you accept a half sack of flour? I have extra, for the baker's dozen you see. I don't make mistakes, so I can make do, and I... I'll give you a sample of my own yeast."

"Done." She rifled through her pack, producing a small vial of green liquid and three fronds of a pointy plant. She removed the stopper on the vile and dropped three tiny drops of the liquid onto the girl's tongue, before handing the vile to the baker. "Three drops of this four times each day." She snapped a piece from one of the fronds and ran it across the girl's brow. "Use these to cool her until the fever subsides." She paused, staring into the flickering flames of the hearth. "If it subsides."

She sat with the baker a while, and they chatted over tin mugs of hot water. The girl tossed and turned on the baker's bed, and whimpered occasionally.

"Fever dreams, most likely," the baker said in a hushed tone. "So, you're the Curator? Now you, I thought you were a myth."

"Far from it. I'm as real as my…" She paused and caught herself. "As The Collection."

"Well, pleased to meet a living legend, and thanks for your help. It seems like she might make it after all."

"Not many would trade for a stranger. Not least a dying one."

"Well, we have to look after the kids, right? Or else, who's next? Now, let me go write down that recipe for you."

"It's getting dark. I'll come back tomorrow afternoon and collect it. Besides, I wanted to go down to the canal, see what they have to trade."

Bargemen were always moving around, like the nomads and gypsy caravans of old. She knew they were likely to have something rare or exciting to trade, and they usually wanted new things to read on their journeys. She'd have to copy some more stories from The Collection.

The baker got up but she held up her hand. "I'll see myself out. You stay with her."

The curator made her way downstairs into the main bakery. The boy was kneading a heavy batch of dough, rolling it back and forth against a large wooden board, his muscles bulging with the effort. He stopped as she entered, standing up straight respectfully.

"Thank you," he said.

"You're quite welcome."

"We lost Mum to a fever. Dad probably didn't mention it. I was scared".

She felt the tears well up at his stoicism and steeled herself. "It's okay, she's okay now."

She stepped out into the bitter evening air, walking with purpose. Back to the main street, now empty apart from the occasional wagon; back to the little alleyway she had come from, identified by the three white marks on the corner. She recited the route to herself: left, right, two lefts, and then a right. She placed a long brass key into the lock and turned it, before stopping dead.

There was a smell on the cold air., She drew it in through her nose. It hung like a memory all about this place. Burnt spices and sandalwood. She dashed inside and locked the door behind her, then ran to the cabinet in which she'd left her loaded long rifle. Slumping down with her back against it, she watched the door, just watching. Watching…

Her eyes snapped open and the floor of The Collection came into view, rays of bright light pouring in from the observatory, giving a chapel-like feel to the place. By her guess it was already late morning. She'd tried to stay awake but clearly she'd failed. Now, clutching the long rifle like a favourite teddy bear, she wondered if she'd simply imagined it.

She washed her face and ate a handful of berries. Not strawberries, but the more common blackberries and redcurrants she had in abundance. Then she strapped on her pack and rifle, and headed back out into the world. As she closed the door there was a loud clatter inside, which she knew to be an objection to not being fed.

"I'll make it up to you," she called through the door, before walking away.

The sun had already passed its highest point, so she knew time was short. She'd tried so hard to stay awake. It must have been the very small hours of the morning when she eventually gave in to slumber. As she turned out onto the main street, it was strangely empty. Carts and stands stood empty, storefronts were shuttered and closed, no crowds busied the streets around her.

At the end of the road, outside what must have once been a church or civic building, a man stood at an improvised lectern, addressing a large crowd.

"Yes!" he cried. "We are doing everything we can, and the mayor wishes me to assure you that your safety is of our paramount concern."

"My husband never came home last night," one woman yelled, tears in her eyes.

"Does that happen often?" a heckler among the crowd cried out.

"Now, now," said the man at the lectern, pressing his ill-fitting spectacles back up onto the bridge of his nose. "That's quite enough of that. What we do know is that sometime late last night, a hound, or number of hounds…"

"Or wolves!" someone interrupted.

"Yes, or wolves, came upon our town, likely from the nearby forest. They attacked, leaving twelve dead and several more seriously injured. We're pleased to say that none of the injured have developed fever or other signs of rabies. Hunters are out seeking the beasts now, and we wish to assure you everything is in hand."

The curator had heard enough. This kind of chaos was all too common and there was little she could do about it. But she slipped her rifle from her shoulder into her hands.

"Just in case," she said under her breath.

She made it down to the canal in good time, the lack of crowds made moving around a lot easier. There were few boats left. She spied one boatman, just about to cast off, and ran over to him.

"Excuse me," she called.

"Yes, miss, what can I do for you?"

"Where did everyone go? The local baker told me this canal was a hive of activity."

"Well, usually that'd be true. We have fish auctions here most days. But after last night everyone just wanted to move along."

"The wolves, you mean?"

"Wolves?" he said quizzically. "Wolves be the least of our problems."

"Whatever do you mean by that? The whole town is looking for them."

"Wolves ain't the only thing were out looking for supper last night," he said, eyes darting side to side as if checking he wasn't being watched. "There were something in the water. Some giant eel or sea snake or something. Dragged one of Stan's boys clean off the boat. Stan saw it and stuck it with a boat hook, but it just slithered away. Couple o' the other lads almost got had too, but they was too fast for it. Naw, you take my word for it, missy, keep that rifle o' yers close and you get outta here quick as ye can. Stay away from the water, and stay off dem streets at night. This ain't normal. It's like a nightmare."

She nodded and thanked the man as he cast his rope off, jumping back onto his boat and heading out into the flows. The curator began striding back up the hill towards town. She would check in with the baker, collect her dues and get out of here. This was getting dangerous, and she'd made no arrangements for a successor. Self-preservation was, she had decided long ago, an essential skill of curation.

"You can't save anyone if you don't survive, 613.6.2," she recited aloud.

It took about ten minutes to find her way back to the bakery. It was closed and shuttered like everywhere else. She knocked on the door and waited. After a minute or so had passed, the baker answered, white as his apron, gaunt almost.

"Come in," he muttered in a raspy voice. "Your recipe and things are in the sack on the table. Everything's there, as promised." He sat and huddled in a chair by the cold fireplace, not looking at her.

"Whatever's the matter? Are you ok? Is it the girl, did she… did she not make it?"

"She made it," he said. "But something happened. I fell asleep, see, I tried to keep watch but it was late and I just…nodded off."

She took a seat on a nearby stool. "Go on."

"When I woke up she was gone. Must have come to in a strange place and been frightened. Wandered off, probably had a home to go to. I woke up when I heard the door slam. Emmet, my boy, I think it was him going after her. He sleeps down in the bakery to get the ovens going early." Tears filled his eyes.

"He didn't come, back did he?" she asked.

He shook his head, and buried his face in his gnarled hands.

She sat with him for a few hours, brewing tea from herbs she had in her pack. Try as she might, she couldn't comfort him. He barely spoke. As the sun dropped below the roofs outside, she knew that she would need to get going. This place was getting more dangerous by the day. She built up the fire and hugged the baker, who looked older than he had been the day before.

"Take care of yourself," she whispered. She wanted to say she was sure Emmet would come back, give him some hope, some ray of light to reassure him. But she'd lived in this cold world long enough, and she refused to lie to him.

She unslung her rifle and stepped out into the street, walking cautiously but with purpose as she'd been taught by her father. The streets were empty. Not just quiet, but empty. A fog was rolling in, as thick as the fear that hung about the place. As she turned into the alleyway she heard a strange sound ahead, like something being dragged slowly along a floor. She walked along the left-hand wall, waiting to see the chalk mark that would tell her when to turn.

Left, then right, two lefts and... out of the fog a set of red eyes darted towards her, open jaw snapping just in front of her face, great teeth of yellowed white. She was knocked to the ground, the rifle flying from her grasp and bouncing over the cold cobbles. The head snarled furiously but was held in check by an invisible leash.

She could see two more sets of eyes behind it now. They were circling her. She reached into her sleeve for her knife but it wasn't there. Why wasn't it there? It was always there, she never removed it. She scrabbled on the cobbles, trying to find her feet, looking around as the sound of heavy dragging grew louder and louder. Perhaps the wolves already had their prey, and were protecting it. Was that it? Had she disturbed them?

She got up, took two steps back and tripped, but not over the rifle. The body of a giant snake slithered back into the fog. She panicked as the red eyes of the wolves drew closer, the sound of drool splashing onto the floor as they snarled and growled. Regaining her feet once more, she ran in the opposite direction, followed not by claws on cobble but that slow dragging sound. She turned right, left... no, wait.

It was too late. The dead end loomed in front of her. She dropped to her knees, gasping to catch her breath as she closed her eyes and waited for the inevitable. There was tinkling sound, of metal on stone. Laying on the cold damp cobbles, was a silver whistle on a chain. She looked behind her to see the red eyes gleaming at the entrance of the cul-de-sac. She gripped the whistle, stood to face them, and blew. Hard.

Nothing. No sound. She couldn't hear anything. The stupid thing was broken. She blew again harder, and again. There was a blood curdling howl, an unnatural sound that shredded the air and stabbed at her ears. The dragging sound echoed around her. Her thumping heart added a hunter's drum to the chaos...

And then they were gone. The fog began to dissipate. The alleyway was empty. She could see the white mark on the corner opposite this one. Heart still thumping, she crept along the dead-end path to the alleyway, then sprinted for the door. Scooping up the rifle on her way past and running down the last, long narrow passage, she didn't stop running until she made it. She slammed the key into the lock, twisting fiercely and taking one last look over her shoulder.

At the other end of the alleyway, walking away from her, she saw a tall man in a dark coat and a little girl in a white dress.

She slammed the door, locking it behind her, and ran to the observatory. Pulling back the curtain, she spun the handle furiously, one, two, three, four. Then she collapsed to the floor and sobbed. What had just happened? Where had she just been?

A loud, rhythmic rumbling echoed through The Collection and a warmth filled her. She smiled faintly and exhaled, for what felt like the first time in an hour. She stood and dusted herself down.

"Okay, I'm coming. I did promise."

But as she walked towards the staircase she stopped dead in her tracks, heart racing. There was a faint smell.

Burnt spices and sandalwood.

FAO: ORDO INGENIARIUM

by Lorraine McKee

Lorraine is an Anglo-American ex-lecturer in Multimedia Technologies who fell off a train platform one day, causing her to have an epiphany. She hated her job. This epiphany then caused her to run away to a field to be an ecologist and she now spends her time in and around sites of infrastructure and construction, looking for amphibians, mammals, noxious plants and interesting fungi, which she then writes technical reports about. When not bothering nature, she engages in playing and running Live Action Role Play events and has an unhealthy interest in folklore.

> Access: File [DIARY 1]
> Access: Granted; Displaying File [DIARY 1]

Screw this. Why should there only be one Collection? Fair enough, the Curator was nice to loan me that book, and I copied it down because I needed my own copy, or at least an approximation thereof [Edit: And have recopied it, sure enough – see File: DIARY 3]. I'll have to share what I got, which I guess is the point, but damn it's a slow process. The book isn't straightforward either, but it is a map of what needs doing and I am set upon my path. This world don't just need fancy stories though. It needs a bigger bully than the rest to keep others in line. It needs engineering and, above all, it needs sanitation and education. I have to do something. Expend this energy. Make things… better. That's the wrong word but I'll stick with it for now. We must build again, and that's different from rebuild. I may be het up because for one thing, the Curator seemed so resigned to just scrape by in The Cold and, well... Meg is the other thing.

I'm running out of paper and thoughts for tonight, but tomorrow I'll go out looking and hopefully I'll find something to do that improves the world.

> Access: File [DIARY 2]
> Access: Granted; Displaying File [DIARY 2]

Oh, I found alright.

What I largely found was people going missing from The Flats. Caught wind of the scam when I was in the bar. This guy Leonard sends a messenger to say that one of the villagers has been kidnapped and if someone comes to present the ransom demands, this villager will be released. Emotion ensued, which didn't help anyone; his friends got angry, his wife was wailing and no one was thinking clearly. So I offered to go see if I could talk this Leonard guy out of his antisocial behaviour and into being reasonable. After all, his name was Leonard; not exactly threatening.

I decided to take Meg with me and, in case she didn't help, my trusty boot knife. I got there and found this poor soul locked away in an old trunk in what used to, by all accounts, be a vehicular wrecking yard. As I was springing him, I noticed there's a couple of spikes about the place festooned with human skulls, and a muffled voice behind me said quietly:

"What are you doing there, friend?"

Friend. Now there's a threat. I turned around ready to tell this guy just that, and I saw a man over 6 and a half feet tall and well over 400lbs in weight, once the armour is accounted for. Bright golden armour, covering everywhere. The freed villager had already run off, so I just stared for a moment before my reply came:

"I guess you must be Leonard."

The armour ignored me and mused out loud. "I could just sit on you, but the stomach and intestinal contents would spill and ruin the meat. Much more fun to grab your head and squeeze. Watch you pop like a watermelon. Ever seen a watermelon?"

"Do what now?" I replied.

"Have you ever seen a watermelon?"

"I'm sorry, what?" I stepped forwards, tilting my head slightly so I could hear him better.

"Have you ever seen a watermelon?"

"I'm sure whatever you have to say would be quite intimidating, but I just can't understand you, sorry."

Leonard ripped his helmet off, exasperated. "Have you ever seen a watermelon?"

He was a forty-ish year old grey man before Meg made contact with his skull. He crumpled. In the war of head vs. bat, bat always wins. No matter how much armour you got elsewhere.

I pulled him out of his suit and decided it might be nice to go for a spin. I was right. Four people came back during the night, cowed with fear, each having been his messengers. I told them, if you'll excuse my language, to fuck off because Leonard was dead. They listened because I had the suit. I went home. Good day.

> Access: File [DIARY 3]
> Access: Granted; Displaying File [DIARY 3]

Spent the day with the suit. Seems it's called a Human Industrial Neutron Deflector or HIND. Sadly, Leonard wasn't the type to have a manual. Can't figure out what keeps it powered, but I think it's probably kinetic energy. It's more than just rad armour - the arm has a display unit and there's file storage here. It seems to have been developed just before the Cold because the thing isn't new. Wish I knew where I could get more, but there were no hints from Leonard's digs. He probably got it a similar way to how I did. Anyhow, I've input the book into the HIND now; also, I can just talk and my diary is written. I'm ok with this, though nothing replaces paper and ink for sharing. But this HIND, it could be a walking library, it could... huh.

The helmet just blipped. A map just displayed inside on the lower left corner and it blinked at me. Guess red dot marks the spot. Too interesting to not go see what that is.

> Access: File [DIARY 4]
> Access: Granted; Displaying File [DIARY 4]

There's a thing called The Mountain. It's got a similar mechanism to The Collection for travelling, I reckon. The Mountain is a facility that homes in on the areas that have some radioactive taint, but are recoverable if you just put the work in. This suit, we think, comes from there originally.

Annie and Jo were nice enough to let me keep the suit on account of us deciding to work together since we have more or less the same goals. They live in The Mountain and keep it going. Annie's an old pre-Cold construction worker who don't know when to quit, bless her heart, and Jo is one of her apprentices and the pilot, for want of a better word. Meg would have gotten on with them well. Probably would have thought Annie to be "brash and crass", but in a good way.

Seems there's an order of folk who work within The Mountain too, but it's so large they hardly meet and they work pretty independently doing the same reclamations. Call themselves the Ordo Ingeniarius, and they seem to be part of a larger organisation. The Ordo recovers land by scraping up contaminated dirt and storing it somewhere inside the facility but they also train people to make the world a better place, usually through doing the dirty work like shifting dirty water away from the clean. Preventing disease. Reclaiming what land and resources we can.

Jo says The Mountain facility is under the Yucca somewhere, and just the doors move. Either way, I've been helping them with their operations because this is what is needed. They're good people.

> Access: File [DIARY 5]
> Access: Granted; Displaying File [DIARY 5]

Today I rescued a pig. Guess that's the kind of operation the HIND is for. For reference, a pig is a bit of engineering equipment used to clear a pipeline. Well, ours was broke, so we scavved some bits from one of the more awful parts of town. Anyhow, Jo fixed it right up and put it into the distributor chute only for it to get stuck. So I ended up going in there as the only person with the equipment to do it. I heard why it was called a pig though because once it unstuck that squealing... I've never heard anything like it. Apparently that meant it was working.

Still, we're back on track for shifting this next heap of muck. Used to have a nuclear power plant near it. That went, big time, but most of the cesium only impacted the first four inches of dirt at this distance. Worst part is that the leaves don't biodegrade here. Something to do with the fungi that used to eat them not existing in these parts any more. That's Gamma for you.

Still, they're in the compactor now and the remnants of the forest have been bulldozed. Hopefully the people can make something better of it. And if they can't, nature can.

> Access: File [DIARY 6]
> Access: Granted; Displaying File [DIARY 6]

You know what angers me about The Collection? All those books and I don't reckon enough of the ones about civil engineering get shared. I mean, most folk get by but people like to live together. That means towns. That means a lot of crap. Now that's fine because in a big town, someone will always prentice up and take a hit for the team to keep the town disease-free. But smaller places may not have the luxury of a civil engineer or their apprentice.

Last place we just came from was the very definition of a shit tip. Excuse my language, but I'm a little ticked. People try to have common sense, but some are stupid and others are just assholes. We did a flush. And by we, I mean me. I feel sorry for the HIND but it's probably cleaner now than it's been for a while, even though it don't feel it. And nor do I because the stench was enough to test my fortitude, in which I am not lacking. Jo used her contacts to get wastewater facilities started here. Hell of a job, but it'll be worth it to make Lux clean again. And hey, the book says it needs doing. So it gets done.

Just wish The Collection would spend more time educating about this kind of thing. They do some, but they need to hurry it along. Set up a school or something. Work out how to make a photocopier work, says Annie. They have all the knowledge. It's up to them to share it out better. I've seen them twice now and whilst I really do appreciate their work, they're always so clean and I don't reckon they do an honest day's hard graft ever, though I may just be jealous. Still, without them I wouldn't have my guide. Just wish I'd had it sooner. If I'd had it sooner, maybe I wouldn't have killed her.

Yeah, I know, I'm being unfair to myself. I got sick and then so did she. I made it. Meg didn't. Ain't my fault. Ain't not my fault.

That's not the point. Those assholes need to educate the masses to save lives, and they ain't doing it fast enough. Guess that's on us to try and remedy.

> Access: File [DIARY 7]
> Access: Granted; Displaying File [DIARY 7]

Annie got pneumonia. She says it isn't pneumonia, but she sure has the symptoms of pneumonia. She reckons it was that building about a week ago that we went scavving in. We needed a fanbelt for her digger. It's old and scarred, but it keeps marching on with a little maintenance, kind of like her. The place was low radiation, so we didn't bother with equipment because we could just take some KI and not risk either the suits or the armour being too heavy for the floor. Lesson learned.

The thing about radiation, even in the places less plagued, is that the people were displaced. You displace the people and nature creeps back in because radiation is less bad for nature than people. The building was filled with pigeons. And pigeons... well, they crap everywhere. Which is fine until you kick it up or part of a building collapses because you meet other scavs who decide to attack an old lady. Scav didn't know what hit her (it was Annie, followed by Meg) and she fell backwards into a not-so-supportive beam. It went. We got out, but the scav didn't make it. The dust cloud that kicked up was chronic. Annie reckons she got something from the pigeon guano. Psittacosis, she says.

I've taken it into my mind to kill every pigeon I happen upon, but I realise that's inefficient. So I've spoken to Jo. She reckons we can set up an aviary and I maybe could barter for some hawks and use them when we find pigeons. Pigeons colonise all the old infrastructure because predators don't tend to survive long in areas with even small amounts of contamination. Nothing's eating them. Seems I can change that.

I hope Annie pulls through. I don't want to see another person die that way.

> Access: File [DIARY 8]
> Access: Granted; Displaying File [DIARY 8]

I wish I knew how the lab works. Penicillin. Amoxycillin. All from what's been discarded. I've heard tell of people who know this stuff, but how much they're sharing, I don't know. Ours is automated and either way, Annie's being treated. There's life in the old girl yet, touch wood. At least I fixed her digger, and hey, if the digger is good, she's got to be too. That's what I keep telling us both, anyway. She's too stub... Huh.

...the hell is that? The HUD in the HIND has just lit up with warnings and my dosimeter just cracked. I'm en route back inside. Jo! You hear me?! This is going to be a full decon. Something's really not right out here. Screw it, Jo, I'm moving at pace and... Something is here. Something is... Fuck. JO, GET READY FOR A QUICK DECON AND CLOSE THAT DOOR BEHIND ME!

> Access: File [DIARY 8.5]
> Access: Granted; Displaying File [DIARY 8.5]

I've never seen the HIND react like that. Only made it into The Mountain moments before... before I don't care to think what. The HIND is still in full decon and I just hope it took the brunt of the radiation. The dosimeter is just there for precaution, but it's going to be a nice few days whilst I sit and wait to see if little red dots show and my hair falls out. We haven't disengaged doorway yet because... we started here. We need to be here. This is an island so it don't have the resources. The people haven't mentioned anything like this so It must be new.

I can hear It. It's making good attempts at pounding the doorway in. Real good attempts because metal shouldn't buckle like that and well, that's getting worrying now. Jo says The Mountain isn't responding to a forced disengagement, so this is problematic. Those doors aren't going to be able to sustain much more.

> Access: File [DIARY 9]
> Access: Granted; Displaying File [DIARY 9]

I lied. It wasn't problematic. I figured if we opened the compactor doors, it'd be drawn to them and fortunately, I was right. Once that thing entered the compactors, Jo was able to close them up and disengage the doors. She makes that mechanism dance for sure, because she re-engaged doors on an underwater city and then opened the compactors. So, uh, whatever it or they were is now deep underwater and unless it's something truly monstrous, it's dead.

I ain't thinking about that part too hard; I'm mostly still feeling smug at our joint effort to rid ourselves of it. Personally, I'm feeling smug about the compactor idea, but I'm glad Jo thought about underwater doors. Something like that inside the inner workings of The Mountain would probably qualify as A Bad Thing.

We're going back to Souda. If there's something else just like it there, we can't leave it. We finish the job.

> Access: File [DIARY 10]
> Access: Granted; Displaying File [DIARY 10]

Today, I nearly died because of my sweater.

Lesson learned: Never leave clothing outside during a dust storm that later turns out to have been a radioactive dust storm. It probably isn't wearable.

Thanks, Annie.

Don't know what to do with it now though. It was Meg's that I took in retaliation for her taking mine. Gods, I miss her. I'll hang it up in decon and see if anything can be done. It may just end up staying in there. I'm not ready to get rid.

> Access: File [DIARY 11]
> Access: Granted; Displaying File [DIARY 11]

Came upon an eerie but tidy settlement earlier today. The mayor was frankly weird. He smiled too much and his clothes were too clean but he seemed friendly enough, especially as I returned his dog to him. Big black Doberman, showed up at our door and wouldn't let Jo or Annie more'n four steps outside. Fierce animal, but that's the good thing about the

HIND. Dog may bite but metal don't care. So I heaved it up and took it back to the mayor where it became so docile it was, again, weird. If it's that well trained around him, I'm not going to complain as long as it stays that way.

We haven't been able to find a reason The Mountain took us here, incidentally, which is kind of annoying. It does this occasionally, sometimes for no reason or sometimes because there's radiation that's really well hidden. So until we figure it out, the Mayor has asked us to dinner. He might be weird but I'm not going to look free food in the mouth. Annie and I are taking him up on his offer, but the Ordo has rules about leaving The Mountain unattended, so we're hoping to get a doggy bag for Jo.

….I think it's a good pun under the circumstances.

I hope she likes curry.

***

Sirs,

The above logs have been copied down from the HIND for investigation by the Ordo.

Please find below my log of occurrences.

~~~~~~~~~~~~~~~~~~~~~~~~~~~~~~

Two days and no return, so I called the Ordo for reinforcements. Their pilot relieved me. Before I made it as far as the village, I saw the HIND standing facing an embankment in the distance. It was motionless and the wearer would not respond. I pulled the helm off and found Annie inside. She was non-responsive at first, but I managed to get her to walk back to The Mountain. I would like to request that she goes to The Hospital for evaluation as she is catatonic by day and screams blue murder at night. This is beyond simple shock. From what I can tell, she was put in the suit to be saved as she doesn't seem to have the will for it herself. Perhaps in time there is something the psychs can do.

I went back and beyond the point where I found Annie. Approximately 300m south, I found a body wearing the sweater from the decon. That was all the body was wearing, save for a band of black fabric melted into the skin across the top of thighs. The body was covered in burns and the nose and lips were missing. I'd forgotten how much skin melts when it is exposed to radiation. It melts a lot. The body was unidentifiable, but I know who it was.

I found a message scrawled in the dirt next to the body. It read "Abandon all hope, ye who enter here."

Dosimeter readings were high and I am uncertain as to how long I was standing there in shock. I do not believe I have been compromised but I

will monitor myself for exposure.
~~~~~~~~~~~~~~~~~~~~~~~~~~~~~~~~~

My recommendations are a 50km exclusion zone around the township of Lethe, reinforced by signage and a bulletin to all Miscellanies on system. Rogue Miscellanies should be notified at first convenience.

I would like to request a temporary transfer to the Kew Miscellany for one year for therapeutic purposes.

Jo
Pilot of Gamma Branch

CAFFEINE FIX

by Natalie Faulkner

Natalie is a management consultant for a Financial Services firm in London. She's also a knight in shining armour fighting against evil, or a space Viking trying to mend her fallen comrades, or a mechanic just trying to keep her ship in the air. Possibly some weird combination of all four. She has an overactive imagination and tends to spontaneously burst into song.

Day breaks over the trees and it isn't long before the forest erupts in a riot of noise. Closer to the ground, the cacophony is added to by the colourful language of a woman as she fights her way out of her tent. Twenty years in this life and she still hasn't learned how to be a morning person.

"Coffee?" a voice calls out.

She turns to him and narrows her eyes. "Only if it comes without that damned chirpy smile of yours."

"I can try."

He hands it over, hiding his smirk with a cough, and there is a moment of quiet as she slowly inhales from the battered cup. Out of everything that had been salvaged from the Cold, this is one of the few things she loves. Fresh coffee, every morning. Grown, dried, and roasted on the small plantation they have carefully cultivated. It's their biggest and best bargaining chip and, out of everything in this infinitely harder life, it's the one thing she wouldn't change for the world.

She savours each sip, feeling the caffeine slowly inject life back into her veins. It's a morning ritual that she's determined not to forget. Her parents, her brother with his wife and kids; a carefree childhood, an idyllic mix of town and country that made her as comfortable with horses as it did with the city bankers that came to her father's ranch. Holidays spent with family before heading to university. Then the call from her father before the lines went dead - America, China and Russia were at war. The nukes fired on the other side of the world, without a care for the retaliation unleashed by leaders so crazed by power that they didn't care who they hurt to get it. The fight to escape from Indiana as the world around her became angry and violent. The trek south, desperate to find something still untouched by the gangs that burned and captured and killed.

She opens her eyes and gazes at what is now home. It's a proper settlement, too large to be called a camp any more. People who found them and didn't move on; others from larger towns that just wanted out and heard the fairy story of a simpler life. They worked hard to keep it secluded and remote but, after twenty years, the rainforest had done much of the work for them. These days it's wildlife rather than raiders that pose the biggest threat. Life could be better, could always be easier, but she's proud of what they've built here.

"Feel like a real person now?"

"Shut up, Harry." She walks off with his laughter ringing in her ears and a smile on her lips.

She's one of the older ones, turned forty over the winter but didn't mention it. Birthdays were never her thing. She's kept a track of the years as they go by, just because it feels like she should.

She wanders around, trying to talk to as many people as she can. She's the mediator, the 'locum' leader because she refuses to be given any kind of title and maintains that they don't actually need someone in charge. But they all look to her and she knows it. Calls of greeting as she walks, hands clasped and hugs exchanged in greeting. It's a community, a family that have found each other.

"Selene!" Jakub, the youngest of them all barrels into her with a bear-hug around her waist and sends them both flying to the ground.

"Monster! What was that for?"

"There's a cat in the falls!"

Instantly she's on her feet and moving. The smiles of those around her change to resolve. They've not seen a big cat in years. Selene's pretty sure they were hunted to extinction once animal fur became one of the best ways to stay warm. But predators are still a very big issues and, whilst Jakub is prone to exaggeration, she won't risk anything. There are weapons enough: crude machetes from old metal fan blades, spears and bows, spades.

They head towards the falls. Jakub follows at her heels, chattering about the cat and how it was simply hanging in the air, sniffing at the waterfall. She's not sure how much to believe him.

When they arrive she can see the crowd chattering to each other by the water's edge. They start shouting as she approaches, pointing at the sheet of falling water. She listens briefly - calls of 'cat' and 'floating door' are all she needs before she motions them aside and walks into the pool.

As soon as she's past the curtain she stops dead, seeing what all the clamour was about. There's a door, or more accurately a space, that shouldn't be there. Light spills out, silhouetting the head of a giant tiger as it laps at the water. When it catches her scent it looks straight at her and growls, low and dangerous.

"Rohini!"

The cat moves and is replaced by a man, older than her, who sits so his legs are in the water, wincing at the cold. He starts to speak, running through different languages. She recognises some but stops him when he gets to Portuguese. Best for him to speak in a language the whole settlement will understand.

"Who are you? Why are you here?" Suspicion is clear in her voice, too easy from years of survival.

"My name is Kostas. I look after the Collection." He spreads his hands, open and unarmed. "We would help you if you need it."

She wants to scoff at this man and demand to know what he really wants. The Collection is a myth, something told to children to amuse and entertain. Not real. But nothing can change the fact that this man is hanging in mid-air with a tiger trying to get past him. So she suspends her disbelief for a moment, lowers her weapon and steps back.

"We don't need your help."

"You don't have any problems with radiation? Farming? Sanitation?"

She shakes her head. "But I can offer you a coffee, in return for your story."

The man's tired eyes go wide before he laughs joyfully. "You my friend, have just made my year. Come, lead on and I will tell you a tale of The Collection."

She grins, his mood infectious. Even in this new world, people love a good caffeine fix.

READER

by Allen Stroud

Allen Stroud is a University Lecturer from Buckinghamshire New University in High Wycombe. He runs the Film and TV Production programme and the new BA (Hons) Creative Writing for Publication. He is currently completing a Ph. D. at the University of Winchester, looking at world design techniques in Fantasy and Science Fiction. He also writes music for audio books and audio dramas and writes Science Fiction and Fantasy stories. He is the journal editor for the British Fantasy Society and Chair of Fantasycon 2017

I don't know where you found this note. I know where I left it, tucked into a book on the corner of a shelf.

It was *Moby Dick* - the last book I read.

I had to leave the note there to mark the end of everything, all that I've learned and experienced from the written word. The account of Ahab's tragic quest is not a summary of my knowledge, but it's significant in being my last story, the last images in my mind, conjured from words that were not my own.

The ocean waves, the storm, the violent conflict between man and whale, the death and obliteration of it all, ending with one survivor, Ishmael, the narrator to tell us the story.

My life was a reverse of this. The ruinous obsession of one man, destroying himself and everything around him, leaving a lone survivor to tell the story, compared to one woman left alone amidst hundreds and hundreds of stories, preserved for lifetimes into an unknown future.

There are more books here than I can comprehend, let alone read. There is something about that which changes how you think about your environment, your world of books, of facts, of fiction. What does it mean, to read and imagine the places in all these stories?

When I first came here, the shelves were a challenge. Despite a conscious calculation that I wouldn't be able to read everything I was still determined to make a dent in the acquired knowledge. I sampled as much and as fast as I could, at times, cursing myself for not taking in the words. I stopped rarely, jamming my mouth with food and water in between chapter. I neglected myself. Who cared if I washed? If I looked my best? Only I remained to judge and I was quickly being carried away into hundreds of different, more exciting places. I became a vessel for all that came alive from the page.

I can't remember many of those stories, I only know what they were because I was systematic, starting on a shelf, going along the titles one by one, following the organised system laid out by some stranger, some hero who saved all these books.

I didn't sleep much back then. I couldn't waste time amidst this amassed written sage. It took a while to get used to making a bed between the shelves, on the floor in the aisle, but that was where I wanted to be. If my eyes would no longer take in the words, perhaps I would absorb them while I slept, some kind of osmosis between paper and skin? I would be a lesser avatar of this god of latent knowledge, waiting for me to unlock each secret in turn.

I awoke in the dark many times. At first I imagined not being alone, as if some stranger had found this place for the first time, discovering me on the floor amidst my reading. Later, I accepted no-one would come. I am the last, until you, my reader. The books were the inhabitants here. I was the guest, the colonist amidst natives. Each time I awoke I thought I heard something - scratching, movement or voices. Had I missed some hidden chatter? A conspiracy between volumes and titles, whinging about me as I slept. The foreigner, the immigrant, who disturbed them from their rightful places, caressed them, groped them. Used them until spent and done, to move on to the next. Did they resent me?

After a year, I took stock. Maybe that little nest of tomes was an achievement, a loyal tribe whose secrets I shared, but it didn't feel like it. I'd explored the place, been up and down the rows for hours and hours. I knew how little I'd managed to read.

Still, compared to the natives I had become powerful. Despite the inadequacies of memory, my accumulated knowledge overmatched each individual text upon the shelf. Only in groups could they claim more power than I and, whilst they glowered from each side, they did not raise arms and leap from their ramparts to war upon me.

At night I revelled in my power. I dreamed of stories that blurred and changed. Frodo Baggins had tea with the Mad Hatter, whilst Helen of Troy took instruction from Joan of Arc in martial and religious matters. Dinosaurs roamed golf courses and waited in train stations while children disappeared to Narnia, to Earthsea and beyond. Politicians learned the limitations of power from Dumbledore, Socrates and Oliver Cromwell. concentration camp prisoners were liberated by Elves and American Indians, who went on to rob banks and cheat at cards. All a magnificent tumbling mess of images conjured from words, given new form in my mind.

I read less. I read at random, picking books from wherever my hands fell, retracing my steps only to find food and water. I carried my sleeping bag and pillow with me, shuffling between the aisles until the light failed. Ledgers and diaries, the accounts of huge corporations and a small family corner shop. I would close my eyes and see numbers in the darkness, as if there were hidden calculations tattooed on my eyelids.

For a time, books littered the floor. Without being systematic how else could I know what I'd read, or find my way back? The discarded volumes lay in a trail, charting my journey through this labyrinth of lore. I was Theseus and they became twine, a link back to my purpose in the early days.

Then I met my minotaur.

I opened my eyes to other eyes, green, with narrow inhuman pupils. There were claws on my chest, digging into my skin, pulsing their grip, hard and soft. I felt owned by the creature, claimed as I lay on the hard floor. I had been caught unawares and would be spared, if I acknowledged my sin. At first I had been the vessel. Now I was Cortez, the conqueror, the returning Quetzalcoatl, subjugating texts as I forced a violent path through their serene Eden. I must mend my ways, the minotaur said in those eyes, and acknowledge I am no master here, no god amidst the conquered print.

I swore an oath, that night in the darkness, with the minotaur as my witness - *I will know my place.*

The next morning I retraced my steps, healing the sick and the injured. Those cast aside were restored to their homes. I gave what care I could to the wounded, treating tears and folds as best I could, but there would always be scars to remind me and them of my transgression.

Forgiveness does not lie in servitude. It remains a gift of the wronged and the hurt. Salvation cannot be earned through atonement, it is a boon that should humble a sinner. A true penitent finds all are victims when they err, there is no victory in causing pain and suffering. The wounds cut into both sinner and sinned against. Forgiveness lies in both places too.

After restitution my true purpose began. I left behind any attempt at conquering this place. I became content to exist here, in a way that these books had learned long before me. I became a witness, a confidante and a sharer of those who chose to speak to me. They made their wishes known by catching my eye as I walked and, when they did, I became their attendant, accepting their wisdom with humble grace.

It is this path I have kept. This precious gift I have learned from reading. It is this act that brings me closest to moments throughout time. I cannot know the mind of each writer, the intention and image given to them and translated through words, but I can glimpse something of it in their art. There is a shared magic between us, spanning the ages. Each book is a portal to that time, that purpose. But each book lives, and colours the connection with something of its own.

There are codes of meaning we three share in our ritual - depictions of places, people and circumstance which bring emotion, elation and tears. I can be asked to think, to be persuaded, to act, to mourn and to celebrate from all that I read. In each of these determinations, the magic is there, tangible, sparkling amidst the words. I am sharing with writer and book, but also I am sharing with others who have been affected. There is a community between us that transcends this lonely existence, denying whatever may lie beyond.

I may sleep alone but my companions are with me, all around me. As readers, they have been where I have been, witness to stories as they suspend their own lives. I see their footprints in each folded page and every bookmark. As writers, I know their words. As characters I know their triumph and suffering. All are part of me, around me, legion, loyal and strong.

Never alone.

You don't need to know what happened to me. I got old. What's left is this piece of paper. It's a tiny piece of me stuck in time, waiting, frozen, for you. We have a relationship now, an intimate thing only writers and readers share. I can't know what you're doing as you read, what brought you to this moment. I can only be this part of it, a catalyst perhaps to how you move forward. I get to encode and plan my part of our union long before you arrive. I can be dominant in choosing words, sentences, themes and more. Perhaps what you read is true; perhaps it isn't. Whatever it is, it remains. Fate and intention chose this as my legacy, my final part given new life on lined paper, with my last pen.

If you are reading this, you have come from the Cold. From beyond the frontier of hope to a moment of reverent pause. You should worship here as I did. Take my oath, or an oath of your own and become a companion to all that you see. This land is fertile with wisdom, with memory and lore beyond any lifetime. Drink from it.

Books mean nothing if they are not read.

CORNERED

by Juliette McAlroy

When she isn't being a writer, Juliette McAlroy is a midwife. And a guitarist. And a nerd who still doesn't own enough books or cats. She has a Masters degree in English and has written two novels, but this is her first step into short stories; she has also written too many songs, a bunch of poems and a laptop's-worth of unfinished projects - including the eight sequels to her two completed novels. She lives near Nottingham in a house full of fox-themed nonsense and LARP kit, is easily identified by her orange hair, gets distracted by forests, and at some point she will have had enough sleep.

I'm looking for Rad.

There are things he needs to know. I don't think anyone else knows I'm here. *We're* here. I haven't seen any other people, except for him. The Collection is my home: I live in 618.2 to 618.8. The books are comfortable. They make me feel safe. I read them a lot. I feel guilty that I can't always wash my hands before touching them. I remember what Uncle Kar used to say when I was little and still at home: clean hands, no biscuits and no taking books outdoors. There aren't any biscuits now.

It's very dusty in 618. I can track my footprints on the floorboards, and I can track Rad's, too. His are slowly, slowly, whitening with more dust. I thought about going outside to look for him, but the front door moved again yesterday and I didn't do it. I didn't turn the observatory handle, nor the little one by the front door, and Rad isn't here to do those things for me. I don't trust the door not to move again when I get back.

If I get back.

And if I don't get back, and he's still here,

(looking for me)

Well, then.

So I've gone out. It's cold, but not like the Cold; it's almost like home, like Aunt Bea's home, where the smell of snow wrinkles the inside of your nose and the pine-scent from the woods burrows into everything and your breath turns into smoke. There is smoke, real smoke, woodsmoke on the air. Not like these days, where all you can smell is the acrid stench of burnt rubber and the sharp strange acidity that never quite goes away. Frost crunches under my feet. I should have worn Rad's boots but what if I took them, and I didn't get back, and he needed them? I can manage a little frost. It's no worse than Alba Iulia in winter.

My world is filled with the music from before the Cold. I don't play. I read scores. But I can always hear a kind of haunting music. I think it's because once I turned the handle and we opened the door and we stepped into an old opera house, and there was a musician sitting alone on the stage, playing to no audience. His cello had been broken and put back together again and bound with skin. He played and we listened.

The music took us away, far away, beyond the bounds of decency, but we were alone, save for that solitary cellist, so it was all right. As we lay on the floor of that black-velvet-lined alcove, Rad said I was like that cello. He doesn't play an instrument either but he would lay his hands on me, silent like a priest, starting where the pulses beat bright and blue in my throat, and he would read over my shoulder,

(those deft quiet hands could wring music from me as easily as it would rain if you twisted a cloud)

and he said I'd sing.

I met him in 793.73 where nothing was real. I wasn't sure he was real to begin with. He gave me a little spinner that he'd made out of something white and smooth and warm. Bone, I think. It has ten sides with numbers on: 1-2-3-4-5-6-7-8-9-10. I liked to stand it on the top point and spin it to make it dance over the floor. I stopped doing that when I lost it down the floorboards. I cried, because I loved it and he'd given it to me, and then I pulled the floorboards up. I found the spinner,

(but I pushed all the floorboards down again very quickly after that)

yes, I found the spinner.

I didn't tell Rad I'd lost it, or what I'd found. But I think he knew, because he bored a hole through the top and bottom points and hung it on a copper chain for me to wear. I've never taken it off. The black colour on the numbers has nearly worn away now, but he scratched them in, first, before staining them.

His handwriting is terrible.

I leave messages for him in the Collection, since he disappeared. I don't damage the books. I was brought up properly, even divided as we were between Connemara and Alba Iulia, and the Collection is so much more – more imposing, more important, but also more homely and welcoming – than even the Batthyaneum Library that Aunt Bea showed me when I was very small. But I leave messages in or close to the books I know he might read.

611-612, because that's obvious, so I leave the obvious messages in there. Where are you. Are you all right? Come home. I'm frightened. I love you. They're so obvious, I speak them all into the books. I don't need to write them. He'll know. He'll hear me.

He has something wrong with his left shoulder. Sometimes it grates. When he turns in his sleep it pains him. I can feel the bone under the skin, overgrown around the joint, too heavy, pushing forward. He laughs and says he is bloody crooked, and I tell him he is now growing discontented with the winter,

(I think he is growing wings)

which was one of Aunt Bea's favourite phrases about the Cold. I sleep on that shoulder because he says the weight of my head and my knotted hair eases the pain. It's a good job he's not left-handed, like I am.

The Collection has some left-handed books. Rad loves 741.4, where they all live. If he can't sleep, that's where he'll be; with the left-handed books. He reads them backwards, curled up long-legged in a corner, humming tunes I don't recognise, wrapped in the thin blanket that I used to use as a bed. I've begged him to take one of the furs but he won't. He says he doesn't get cold,

(and oh and oh he is always warm)

as he turns his colourful pages backwards, smiling.

I remember the first time we did that, the first time he drew my head down onto his shoulder where it belonged. There's a place outside that we found, the first time we ventured outside together, when Rad turned the handle and opened the door. A wide open space, a once-green place, surrounding a black leafless oak tree and the wreck of an old sandstone house. That house was like a ship, half-sunk to the left in the bitter acidic earth, as though it had slid too far along the grass and got beached backwards.

We named that broken-down old house as though it were our own. I called it Abbeydale after the house in Connemara. Rad called it The Ruin, because that was what it was, but he found a scorched old plaque, etched with the rain, that said it had once been the House of the Locks. A laser-house, he said. It didn't look locked and I couldn't see any lasers. I looked it up in History when we came home to the Collection. Loques: rags that lepers used to apply to their sores. A lazar-house, where people had once gone to die, pretending they were getting better,

(I have always found it easy to pretend)

and to be with other people like them.

We lay on the grass, or what was left of it, under that black tree, my head on his shoulder, his arms around me, and we looked up into the expanse of oily, pitchy sky that Uncle Kar told me had once been dotted white with stars as though someone had flicked their paintbrush at it. Now there was only ash-black, and the tree itself was hot to the touch. I think the rain had poisoned it. The sky looked just the same from the observatory, when we went home.

I leave metal messages in 355 in case he needs to go to war. There are weapons here, and I bring them to this floor, this section, and leave them lying on the books. They won't hurt the books. They can't. But if he needs them, they are here. He can change them, heat them in a fire, put them together. He could do that. He's clever. He knows people, bodies, he knows how they work. Knowing how weapons work would be child's play.

There's a different war in 930.04916, a much older war, with people making balls out of other people's brains, and queens leaving a layer of destruction on the ground that burned so far down that they're still finding bits of it today, and chieftains jumping out of chariots and tying themselves to trees so they could die properly. I used to like to read other languages in that section, strange sticks running up and down lines, all angles and sharp corners. I showed him the crosshatching and he closed the book in my hands, told me not to look at them. But I've seen him in there, reading about swords and shields, and in his mind I know he is striding over open fields, green fields, leading people into battle, spear in hand, painted as blue as the sky should be but isn't. Maybe I'm at his side. I could be. I'd follow him,

(anywhere)

into battle.

Rad said my hair was called loques, too, or maybe locks; thick knotted plaits that he couldn't get his fingers through, although it didn't stop him trying. I'd never seen anyone else with red hair like me. Uncle Kar said he was a strawberry in his youth before it all went white, but I'd never seen anyone else like me.

But there was Rad: baltic amber, the sands of Luxor at the Theban Necropolis, red honey – 'mad honey' – made from the white rhododendrons up in the Himalayas before all the bees died. Like the old coins you sometimes saw in the barter-market. Not the ones you used to pay for things with, if you were lucky enough to have coins. The old ones. The *round* ones.

Rad liked the round ones. Curves in general, really. Don't go near the corners, he said. I wasn't sure where all the corners were; I looked on the map on the wall by the coat rack but every time I looked at it I saw something different.

I only ever had a coin once. Not a round one. A useful one. It was cold and ugly but it was gold. I took it to the market and pretended to myself that I had ever so many. I eventually gave it to a beautiful, joyous man with tangled hair and heavy-lidded eyes who looked like one of the Pharaohs from 932. He had a book in his silk jacket pocket,

(you weren't supposed to know it was there)

he did. A woman in shapeless brown silks was cooking something over a fire in an old hubcap suspended on chains from a metal spider. I thought she was his sister because they had the same hair but he didn't look at her like his sister and he called her Sweet Nahab in a soft voice. There was a big rat under her skirt,

(oh I saw its tail and its little hands)

but I didn't think she cared. She heard my stomach growl and I tried to hide it by pressing on it, but she gave me a little cupful of the meat and blood and herbs from her silvery pot. It was delicious. I tried to eat it slowly and delicately like Aunt Bea always did, as though I were kissing my fingers to the cook, which is what Uncle Kar used to say. I felt so guilty that I couldn't save some for Rad but I'd never have got it home. Someone would have taken it, it would have gone cold, or I'd have spilled it, and I'd have had to have taken her cup, too.

She told me the recipe but I've never been able to make it myself. There's a garden in the basement but I don't use it much. I get by on water and whatever I can barter for. Dried hare meat. Protein bars. I have used some of the vegetables but I always replant something, thanks to 635, and I never take more than I need.

The beautiful man took my coin, in the end. I thought he was taking it in exchange for the food but the lady said no, that was a present. So he asked me what I wanted and I took a polished amber-glass bottle of thick oil that looked like the night sky and smelled like smoke.

I gave it to Rad. Not all at once. Bit by bit. Drop by drop. In darkness thicker than the oil itself. Hidden behind stacks of books. Balanced on the softness of furs. My hands work it into the curve of his shoulder where the bone has grown too far over the joint. Where his wings are growing. He sighs, almost a groan,

(when he thinks I can't hear him)

and he smiles.

I go to 685 where the books smell of what they talk about. Their bindings are soft and smooth. Rad once traded for furs so that I had a bed. He said they were hound furs. I've never seen a hound outside of 636.7 except for once, and that wasn't up close, so I wouldn't know if that's true. He made me a coat of leather, although that's long gone now, with bartering and general wear. They cut it away in strips, piece by piece, and that's how they took it from me. Hound-skin, Rad said, and he'd dyed the inside of the hood red to match my hair.

I write tiny questions for him in 810. He'll know the answers. I don't write on the books. That would be awful. I write on the shelves, in minuscule letters. Rad says my writing has no business being so pretty. I write fast. It feels strange to hold a pen again. There is ink in the Collection, too. I only ever use the red colour. That way he'll know it's me. I like section 810 a lot. I don't always understand why it makes Rad smile, but it does. And that smile is glorious. The prohibited books in 098 also used to make him smile, but in a different way, and I could tell why some of them were prohibited,

(oh his smile should have been prohibited)

Aunt Bea would have torn some of those books to shreds if she'd seen me reading them, Uncle Kar or no Uncle Kar.

Rad never smiles in 770. Sometimes I find him sitting in there looking at the blank, black, flat screens. They don't do anything, but his hands rest in the air like he's holding an open book. Most of the time he doesn't even have his eyes open. Sometimes his hands move. Sometimes he says things I don't understand. Avatar, live-stream, ten windows. We have a lot more than ten here. When I ask what he means, he says he's remembering how to remember to play before he forgets how to remember.

776 brought forth a pool of flat silver circles, like mirrors. They sparked rainbows if you turned them the right way. Rad found them first; he said he was looking for games, but I couldn't see how you could play with them. I dropped one because I was twirling it on my finger to make the light flash over it, and it broke. He bored holes through the pieces and strung them on a net, and hung it above where we sleep.

Rainbows.

They turn and swing if I touch them.

I remember the first thing he brought me, something he'd traded for: like an apple, but not an apple. I had this mouse, once. Grey with brown ears. Before Rad. When there was just me. It nibbled a hole right through my dress in the night. Nibbled one of my locks clean off my head to make a nest. I think it was trying to make a nest in the books. Well, this not-an-apple was like a baby mouse to touch but when you peeled the skin away inside it was like slithery wet soap.

Rad said he wanted to split the mouse-apple with me; when he split it in two with his knife there was a gnarled, veiny little rock inside and we had to pull the flesh away from it. It broke in half when he set his knife to it, and a seed fell out. I thought it was an almond. I'd tasted almonds before; dry, gritty, until you warmed them, and then they were wonderful. We buried the seed in the garden in case it would make more. And then we ate the flesh, tiny piece by tiny piece, together; it smelled and tasted like a cross between raspberries and roses.

I miss having roses; all of Aunt Bea's roses died when the Cold came. I was too little to remember them properly, but I remember the smell of them. Rad knows what they look like, he told me I was like one; he found pictures of them for me in the Collection and showed me, and then he said no, not a rose, an orchid, and he showed me that, too. I was embarrassed, people don't say things like that to you in Alba Iulia,

(Rad says things I'd never heard)

but the whole world is watching you, he said, here in the Collection, the whole world is here, and that's when he made my name: Shifra Watchworld. I liked it. I kept it.

In 398 I leave drops of blood for when the old tales come creeping and he can't remember me. They look like little poppies on the paper. I read about poppies in 940.3 and 940.53; people used to wear them, because they grew in the mud, and then later on people scored them into their bodies in protest against the Cold.

Admission: I do put the blood on the books. I don't think it hurts them. It's only a drop. I think they like it. It's warm. Like them, I don't cope well with the Cold,

(he is so warm)

but I'd had to go out to find Rad. So I'd shaken the dust off my feet, turned the handle and stepped out.

I could do with that hound-skin coat now. Or even some of our furs. But I will be warm again, I will, when I find him. I am already growing warmer as I think of him. Like an invisible coat. When I think of him I walk differently. I'm taller. Uncle Kar would say I swagger like a bold girl.

When Rad's acting playful he says he'll file me in 133.4 with the witches. But in seriousness he says I'm more like some of the women in Class 8. He murmurs foreign names, names I don't know, into my locks when he's feeling lascivious: Viola, Artemisia, Hermione, Capable, Mercy. At first I was upset because I thought they were his women. Other women. He says they're all me. He explained how. But I've never been up to Class 8. He has.

Once, after we'd bartered for a half-bottle of sweet apple wine, which he doctored with some kind of clear spirits he'd found the last time we opened the front door, he confessed that when we first met he thought I was like the women in 398.2. He told me a story about a girl who went walking in the forest, taking cake to her aunt's house. Her red hair made a great hound follow her through the woods. The hound killed and ate her aunt, and it talked to the girl, dressed up in her aunt's clothing, because he thought her hair was red with blood. He pulled one of my locks when he said that,

(he smiled)

but hounds don't talk.

There's a cat, though. Here. A big one. Greying, but I think it was once reddish like me. Like Rad. I've seen it. Once. When I went down to the basement, to look at the garden. When I saw the blackberries. It was in the shadows, swishing about, and for a minute I didn't think it was real. I froze. It looked so soft I could have slept in its fur but it had knives on its feet and it would have been as big as me if it stood on its hind legs. Maybe bigger. I'm tall, nearly as tall as Rad, but it would have been taller. I wanted to call out to Rad but I didn't dare because my voice might have scared it or annoyed it,

(then he was there oh he was there he was there)

and I heard Rad behind me and he hissed at it. Issst-ashaaa, he said, and it didn't like it, and it backed off and left me alone. It slunk away into the Collection, and Rad held me to him til I stopped shaking, and I haven't seen it since then. But it's still there. It must be still there, somewhere.

In 784.498 I leave the scent of musk oil, my precious perfume; it is in the tiniest bottle. The size of a blackberry with a sliver of cork stopping the neck. There are blackberries in the garden, but only a few; so few I don't dare take one in case anyone notices it's gone. In the same way I use barely any of the oil in 784.498. I don't want to damage the books with it and I don't want the scent to reach anyone else. If there is anyone else. I traded a knitted blue shawl and Aunt Bea's garnet earrings for this oil,

(the very next day I met Rad)

so it means a lot.

Soon, though, I will need to spend much more time in 618.4. I've known that for some time now, and I'd have known it even without my clothes tightening, without the 'tell-tale heart', that quickening. He has to be told.

So I'm looking for Rad.

Behind me, a trail of droplets like poppies blossom on the snow as I walk, and as I turn the corner I can hear a hound breathing.

COMPOST
by Niamh Carey

Niamh has been sharing her wry (and occasionally macabre) take on rural life since before she could read. Early intervention was required to teach her that oral storytelling while sat in the middle of tiny, tractor infested country roads was a poor life choice. She still believes in taking her readers (or LARP participants) out of their comfort zones, or subverting them altogether. She grew up in Co. Laois and currently lives in Dublin.

The Curators are here again. They last came when I was a girl, strange and terrifying in their masks and creaking clothing, and their lilting way of speaking. I could never make out what they were saying, so crowded they were with the elders of the village. Shouting, bartering, begging, accusing sometimes. Where did they go, why did they not take us with them, what use did we have for what they tried to sell? Before I was born, they traded for scrap and salvage. Today they trade for food and things we have made, and what they bring? Magic. Their blessings bring us prosperity, or what passes for it in these parts. Crops that grow, children that live. What more proof do you need?

As we grew up, we heard that they lived under the hills, in a cave at the centre of the world. Some said they flew from the heart of the Cold, a land so badly ravaged that no man could walk its paths and live. Of course, we never travelled far anyway – there was a whole blasted world out there that we'd never seen but the few travellers we met spoke about in hushed tones. The Curators, a magic repository of knowledge. Rumours flew of a strange beast that stalked their every move, of unfathomable powers and some even – when they were drunk and could hold their tongues no longer – suggested they'd released the Cold, started the War. Today they blink surprise at my distended belly and bring me a seat. The children sent away, the trade negotiations begin. Salt harvested from the sea, for information on fertilizer; blood moss in exchange for a copy of the alphabet, painted onto a long strip of metal. So on and so on.

We speak for a few minutes about me, what to expect, and a discussion about the health of the children around here springs up. The Curators draw back a little, anxious to be gone, and I find myself wondering what business they have asking about our babies. Mamó comes up behind me, rubbing my shoulders lightly. She's always known my moods, better than my mother, better even than myself, and her gnarled hands calm me down. A dull cramp rolls through my core and I wince. I'm close to time now. The fear wraps around my spine, settles in my hips, closes my throat. I ask Mamó where my husband is.

"Soon, Nessa. He'll be back soon. He won't miss this."

The Curators stand to leave and one hands me a package. She smiles nervously. They put their bags on their shoulders and begin the walk back to their mysterious home. We follow them with our eyes and, afraid of scrutiny, I tuck away the gift until I am alone. It contains the most luridly coloured roots I have ever seen, and a little sachet of seeds. I eat the roots, their vivid orange glowing in the grey of my home. I imagine what it must be to grow such large, straight things, with no risk of the rot, the grey sludges and the soil that needs to be worked and worked and worked to feed us. The lessons from the Curators' last visit have helped, but to make bone and blood meal we need fuel, and to get fuel we need to trade or grow. We make do for now with a foul compost of rotted seaweed and our own shit. The Curators brought plans this time, showing how to make biofuel with the slurry we use for fertilizer. If we can get that working, we'll be in a much better position.

I am digging rotted seaweed, painstakingly hauled from the coast and up the river, into my garden when the water breaks. As I've been taught to do, I hold myself still and wait for the flow to ease, and look down at the ground. Clear. Just water. A good start. I call my husband and he stands behind me, wraps his hands around mine on the spade, and together we finish digging. A painful tradition but symbolic. Together we make our garden; together we made a home and claimed a scrap of warmth out here in the Cold; together we will realise our greatest joy or worst horror. He takes my arm and helps me, one shuffled step at a time. I desperately want to sit down, curl up around my belly, but we have too much to do before I can no longer walk.

First, to the shrine in the centre of the settlement. A cracked and stained statue of a woman. Robed, crowned in stars, arms spread, standing on a snake's head. We take blades, nick our hands, and drip blood onto her feet. A prayer to the Virgin and the Schoolgirl, and back we go to the house.

As he unrolls tarpaulin and sets up the cot for me on it, I notice for the first time that his hair is thinning. At least it's a thinning at the temples, not great handfuls like Daideó, and his teeth are firm in his head.

I stagger – the contractions are strong, my child is coming. He helps me onto the bed. Up off the bed. I am restless. I convince myself that if I keep moving I won't dwell on my fears. I see the packet of seeds, and think about the Curators.

A little learning is a dangerous thing
Drink deep or taste not the Pierian spring
There shallow draughts intoxicate the brain
and drinking largely sobers it again

They aren't always welcome here. I remember times when the knowledge they brought was no help, or came too late for someone in the village. We had just lost my father from a cut that went rotten when they came and taught us how to cauterise and suture wounds. Small use to him, pushing up the plants, and the memory fresh enough that they were not even offered a meal for their troubles. Yet nobody dared to run them from our gates. We were afraid, I suppose. Afraid our uncanny protectors would abandon us to the banshees and the púca, the strange lights in the bog and the quiet ways. We drink up their knowledge, understand as much as we can and use what we dare. And mostly, it keeps us safe. We wear iron, and ward our houses, and burn a coal over a newborn's bed. We bleed on statues and grind our dead for fertilizer in the hope that it will restore the soil, undo the damage the Cold brought. We wait, even though we despair, for the Curators to teach us more.

I howl in good and earnest.

When Mamó comes in it is as my midwife, not my grandmother. She rattles out instructions to Liam. Whey-faced, he boils water, makes sure that we have clean cloth and the precious bar of soap we traded from the Curators last year.

The day drags on. I can't stand any more. I squat, or sit, or lie on my side. The dread is building.

I huddle in the corner of the tarpaulin and tell the child fairy stories from my childhood. I'm named after Nessa, a mythical queen and the mother of a mighty hero. When it came close to her time, her labour beginning, she was told that if she held on for one more day her son would be born on an auspicious hour. She sat in the river, straddling a flat rock to hold the child inside her until the dawn came. Lying on the cot, with plastic sheeting underneath to catch everything that passes from me, I envy that girl her rock. Mamó lifts my shift and looks between my legs. A grim nod, and Liam smiles reassuringly to me. I tell the child the names I have picked out: Conor for a boy, Ann for a girl.

The shadows grow longer and the beast rises within me. Animal roars and cries rip from my throat, hoarse and likely to crack soon. Mamó makes me turn onto all fours and looks between my legs. She tells me it's not long. To breathe, to control it. I want the rock. I want to stop this. I'm not ready, I can't do it. Too late for that, girleen, it's happening, now pant, pant, pant and relaaaax...good girl.

I am not a good girl, I think. I curse Mamó, I curse my husband, I utter curses I didn't know I had in me, and I squat and I sweat and I pant, pant, pant, relaaax.

The year that Da died, the Curators taught us how to distil a strong liquor that worked better than soap for keeping wounds clean. Or hands that might be touching vulnerable places, for that matter. It is difficult to make, and takes a long time, and we use it sparingly. No midwife's apron is complete without a flask and Mamó was no exception. She takes it out, shakes it to hear the slosh, mimes taking a swig. Knowing that a drop of it could blind you and a bottle kill you stone dead lends a grim humour to the gesture.

The night is long and longer yet. I am beginning to think this child will never be born. On all fours, I bear down and Mamó cries out and Liam's eyes flood with tears. I collapse on my belly. A thin ragged cry – A girl, a girl, a beautiful little girl! - and Mamo places the little scrap on my chest as I shake and weep in relief. My head is light, my heart is lighter, she looks perfect.

The afterbirth is next, I know. That's what the tarp is for. To catch it, dry it, grind it into compost. We waste nothing, not even ourselves. I smile at Liam and he pushes my hair out of my eyes. The baby is quiet now, cuddled up to me while she calms. I feel myself opening again, push out and hear a slithering smack.

It's done. I drift into a doze and think about nothing in particular. My baby, washed at last and wrapped in something soft, nuzzles my breast and latches. The cramps continue but that's no surprise after the day I've had. I'm ready for sleep when I catch a glimpse of Liam's face. A look of naked, raw fear, quickly suppressed by a smile which rips away like a cloud in a gale.

"What's wrong? Mamó?"

My tongue is heavy and my lips are numb. It must be the drink... which I've not tried. I try not to think about it as Mamó, her face stony, kneels between my legs and gets back to work. She reaches for bloodmoss, for her flask, and for things I can't see. She stands. I see her hands and knees are stained red and tears track her face. She backs away and shakes her head. I try to stay calm but all I can think is that I need a coal. A coal for the baby's bed, and what would I need to trade with the strangers for that? My name? My memories? What do they take for the protection of a child? My vision clouds, and clears, and I see them again. Looming from the corner, stretching gloved hands, reaching for my daughter. I cry out, though my voice is weak and hoarse.

"Take me! Take me, not her!"

They laugh and the dark descends.

FOUNDING FATHERS

by Ben Burston

I am the killer of small creatures, flying or scampering, singing or squeaking. I am bloodsoaked, befanged and beclawed. I am sleek and black and wise with age. I have a castle and I live at the top. I sleep little and often. I squire queens, though have no kittens that I know of. My leg is twisted and I have wounds from battles with my rivals. I am older now and must use guile to best the youngest of them. I am the killer of small creatures. Ben is the god-servant who feeds me. I sleep by him some nights. He can do almost anything, but he cannot hunt.

There are 332,897,567 books in the Collection. They sit on 1676 miles of shelves, on 279.3 miles of bookcases. I didn't count them. You couldn't, not if you lived to be fifty. There are 31,536,000 seconds in a year, and you need to sleep and eat and go to the toilet. And it took me the first eight years of being here to learn to count, so they were wasted.

Well, not wasted. You need to know how to count to find out how many books there are. But I didn't count them. I used Mathematics, which I learned from the first bookshelf, Fifth level. But you can't learn that until you've learned to read, which wasted more of those eight years. Well, not wasted exactly. I learned how to read because whoever was here before me left out the right books from 372.4, Third level. Whoever it was must have been very clever, because you can't just take any old 370 books and expect someone to learn. You have to have the right books, in the right order. I can see that now. I couldn't back then.

Abraham Lincoln taught himself to read. He did this to avoid chores. He ended up on hundreds of thousands of tiny pictures called Dollars. I have some. Just like the other dollarmen; Washington, Franklin and Bush. Lincoln is number 5, but that doesn't have any relation to Natural Sciences. The numbers on the Dollars are not related to the numbers in the Collection. I taught myself to read and I taught myself mathematics. And I taught myself to write, obviously. If you can read this then I was successful. Assuming that you can read, of course. I think I've taught myself to speak but I don't have any way in which to tell.

There is a connection between the dollarmen and the Collection though. I found it out after ages of searching. The man who started the Collection - the smaller half (only slightly smaller) - was a dollarman too. His name was Thomas Jefferson. He's number 2. His part of the Collection started with his Library of 6,487 books. The dollarmen were the rulers of the United States of America. The United States of America had an enemy called Great Britain. Great Britain burned the first Collection of The United

States of America hundreds of years ago. So The United States of America purchased dollarman Jefferson's Library for 23,950 dollars. The other half of the Collection, the slightly bigger half was the enemy library, the Great British one. I'll write about that tomorrow.

I didn't count the manuscripts (so this doesn't count), or the tapes or the microfiche or the disks, or the paintings, or any of that. Just the books.

ABOUT THE COLLECTION

Back in October 2016 I had a dream about an abandoned post-apocalyptic library. The ceilings were high and crumbling, the shelves long and full of dust. On a table by the door was a note: 'If you make it here, please look after the cat'.

In November I turned that dream into a 12-part story, posted daily on my blog. The amount of internet traffic went through the roof and a friend asked if he could write a sequel. That sequel became *Shadows in the Light* by Ed Gray (page 37).

Then another person asked.

And another.

So I invited all interested parties to a Facebook group, put up a couple of guidelines about the setting, and sat back.

This anthology is the result of a creative outpouring that was never planned. Some of the contributors were already creative writers; some of them would not previously have claimed to be. But they all found a story in the Cold, and they all believed in The Collection. We hope you do too.

What you hold in your hands started as a dream.

Dreams let us imagine something better.

AC Macklin

18680014R00092

Printed in Poland
by Amazon Fulfillment
Poland Sp. z o.o., Wrocław